"Wade, could I ask you one small favor?" Bronwynn said. *"I really can't get out of this dress. Could you possibly undo me?"*

Wade froze as she presented her back to him. At least forty round pearl buttons ran in a line down her elegant back, holding the back of the beaded white satin wedding dress together. He swallowed hard, his palms sweating.

"Sure," he muttered, but his fingers were shaking as he fumbled with the first tiny button. As buttons and loops went their separate ways, an ever widening V of pale, creamy skin was exposed to his gaze, softer and smoother than the satin dress. Her perfume rose alluringly, tempting him to lower his head.

Bronwynn trembled. His fingers plucking open her dress were sending currents of electricity through her. The heat of Wade's breath on the back of her neck poured over her, melting her knees until she could barely keep from falling back against him.

"There," he said a hoarse rasp. "All done."

"Thank you," she breathed. "I really . . ." Her words trailed off as she looked at Wade. The expression in his eyes was fierce, and a muscle in his cheek twitched, showing he was fighting an inner battle. When he leaned down and took her mouth with his, she wondered if he'd won or lost. . . .

WHAT ARE *LOVESWEPT* ROMANCES?

They are stories of true romance and touching emotion. We believe those two very important ingredients are constants in our highly sensual and very believable stories in the *LOVESWEPT* line. Our goal is to give you, the reader, stories of consistently high quality that may sometimes make you laugh, sometimes make you cry, but are always fresh and creative and contain many delightful surprises within their pages.

Most romance fans read an enormous number of books. Those they truly love, they keep. Others may be traded with friends and soon forgotten. We hope that each *LOVESWEPT* romance will be a treasure—a "keeper." We will always try to publish

LOVE STORIES YOU'LL NEVER FORGET
BY AUTHORS YOU'LL ALWAYS REMEMBER

The Editors

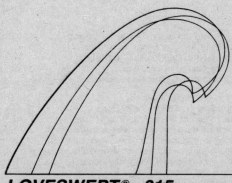

LOVESWEPT® • 315

Tami Hoag
Mismatch

BANTAM BOOKS
TORONTO • NEW YORK • LONDON • SYDNEY • AUCKLAND

MISMATCH
A Bantam Book / March 1989

If you would be interested in receiving protective vinyl
covers for your Loveswept books, please write to this address
for information:

Loveswept
Bantam Books
P.O. Box 985
Hicksville, NY 11802

ISBN 0-553-21982-0

Published simultaneously in the United States and Canada

Bantam Books are published by Bantam Books, a division
of Bantam Doubleday Dell Publishing Group, Inc. Its trademark, consisting of the words "Bantam Books" and the
portrayal of a rooster, is Registered in U.S. Patent and
Trademark Office and in other countries. Marca Registrada.
Bantam Books, 666 Fifth Avenue, New York, New York 10103.

One

"If anyone here today has a reason why these two people should not be joined in holy matrimony, may they speak now or forever hold their peace." Reverend Fitzhumme gave the wedding guests a cursory glance, just out of habit. The bride remembered he'd told them at the rehearsal that in his twenty-seven years of performing marriage ceremonies no one had ever spoken up, though he'd been certain a great many had held their peace—if not forever, at least until the reception.

"Reverend?" the bride asked softly, while all eyes in the church were trained on her and her future husband. She ran a slender hand over the skirt of her white satin gown and tucked a stray strand of her flame-colored hair beneath the cap of her veil. "May I take a moment here, please? I have something I'd like to say."

The groom turned and looked down his aquiline nose, his dark brows drawing together in annoyance. "Bronwynn, what are you doing?" he whispered.

She beamed a smile up at him. "I just have a few thank-yous I'd like to say now, Ross."

He sighed impatiently. Reverend Fitzhumme gave his permission with a motion of his hand.

Bronwynn turned and looked out at the assembled guests. An eerie calm had settled inside her, as if her mind had flipped off all the switches that worried and wondered and made decisions. Her gaze settled on no one person, but scanned the faces and hairstyles and ridiculous hats of the men and women of Boston's upper crust. A brief stab of pain penetrated her heart when she saw the empty pew where her parents would have sat had they lived to see this day. It was just as well they weren't there, she thought as her gaze homed in on her cousin Belinda.

"I would like to take this opportunity to thank you all for coming today," Bronwynn began calmly. A genuine smile lit her face as she saw her sister Zane's worried look. Zane sat in the first row of pews next to her daughter, Rebecca, who had become bored with the role of flower girl and toyed with the lace trim along the edge of her petticoat, unconcerned with the proceedings. "I would like to thank my sister, Zane, for all her help in planning this wedding, but most of all I would like to thank my cousin, Belinda Hughes . . ."

In the third row Belinda's pretty face dropped.

". . . for being so unspeakably contemptible as to sleep with my fiancé two nights before my wedding, thereby showing me just what kind of a despicable, lowlife, money-grubbing scum he really is." She turned and thrust her bouquet of white roses and trailing English ivy into Ross's hands. His face was as white as the flowers. Bronwynn's eyes sparked fire for the first time in days. "Ross Hilliard, I'd have a sex-change operation before I'd marry you!"

"This property is ideal, Murph. There must be three hundred acres of rolling fields and woods. There's a ramshackle old house, but nobody's lived there for years." Wade Grayson paced back and forth in front of the deep green sofa, the telephone dangling from the long fingers of one hand while he held the receiver to his ear with the other. Across the comfortable living room a big yellow Labrador sprawled by the stone fireplace watching his master pace.

"Sounds great, Wade, but I thought we sent you up there for R and R, not to investigate business ventures for the two of us."

He set the phone on the pine coffee table, picked up a bottle of antacid and took a swig. The stuff was actually beginning to taste good to him. The thought sent a shudder through his body as he lit a cigarette and took a long drag.

"Sure," he said, grinning as he flashed the even white teeth that had won over more than one female voter, "but why waste an opportunity? We've been looking for a spot for three years. I was walking by this place yesterday—it's less than a mile down the road from here—and it hit me how perfect it would be. I could see it all—a comfortable lodge, miles of cross-country ski trails. If you're interested in making the investment, I'll check into it. What do you think, pal?"

By the time he hung up Wade was ready to take another long walk down the dirt road that wound back through the trees. He'd been in Vermont trying to relax for three days, and he still was strung tighter than a new tennis racket. His nerves hadn't even begun to unwind. He couldn't quite remember what it was like not to be tense.

A few uninterrupted weeks of peace and quiet were supposedly a reward for having worked countless sixteen, eighteen, even a few twenty-four-hour days to push his clean-water bill through the House before Congress had adjourned for the summer. He found his position as one of Indiana's representatives fulfilling in many ways, but it took its toll on him emotionally and physically. Lord, he thought, his drive and ambition had warped his thinking to the point that he looked sideways at the offer of a vacation. But, then, he realized, he never had been one for lying around. He was a doer. Relaxation made him nervous. He was haunted by the idea that while he was busy relaxing, other people were getting things done.

However, when Dr. Jameson, his physician and good friend, had handed him the key to his vacation house in Vermont and told him to go or else, Wade had accepted. Even though he had felt compelled to get back to his district and in touch with his constituents, common sense and his doctor had prevailed. He wasn't going to be any good to anybody lying in a hospital with a bleeding ulcer.

His shoes kicked up little puffs of dust as he walked down the road with a purposeful stride that should not have belonged to someone on a vacation. In the west the summer sky was ablaze as the sun reluctantly slid down on the other side of the Green Mountains. Behind Wade, Tucker the Labrador dragged himself along, his body language clearly saying he had been perfectly content lounging on the plush carpet by the fireplace, chewing on a rawhide toy.

They turned in at the break in the trees that led back to the old house they had explored the day before. Wade's gaze fastened on the dilapidated, old Victorian house that had once been painted pink. At one time it must have been a grand home with its turret and fancy gingerbread trim, he thought, but its day had come and gone long ago, and he easily could picture a cedar and stone ski lodge in its place.

It wouldn't be a huge resort. They would keep the number of skiers down so the trails wouldn't be crowded.

It would be a great investment and a great place to get away to when the pressures of government started turning his stomach into a blast furnace. Relaxation wasn't so bad if he could ski and make money while he was at it.

"And take that, Ross Hilliard, you incomparable louse!"

Wade stopped in his tracks at the sound of a woman's voice followed by a loud pounding noise. Tucker sat down and leaned heavily against his master's legs, trying to muster a growl. It came out sounding more like indigestion. The woman rounded the corner of the wraparound porch, her brilliant white wedding gown hiked up to her knees, wads of material bunched into her right hand. Wedding gown? he wondered briefly as he watched her. In her left hand she carried a hammer, which she let fly at a large brown suitcase on the top of the porch steps. Never taking his eyes off her, Wade moved into the trees along the drive and tried to work his way closer without calling attention to himself.

Bronwynn charged up to the luggage with the old hammer she'd found. She gave the lock on her erstwhile fiancé's suitcase a vicious whack and then another, all the while calling him every name she could think of. Anger had spurred her on all day since her announcement at the wedding, and it was showing no signs of running out. After she had found Ross out she had wandered around like a zombie in shock, not able to think of what she should do. Finally she had snapped out of the trance. Now she made no effort to calm herself. She deserved to be furious. She deserved to go berserk. She gave the suitcase another smack, springing the lock.

Staring at the contents, she realized there was something else she hadn't known about Ross, he didn't know how to pack a suitcase. All his expensive, tailored clothes had been mushed into a wrinkled mess, and in among his underwear he had packed a bottle of cod liver oil.

"Uck! Yuk!" Bronwynn wrinkled her nose in distaste. "I should have asked to see him pack a suitcase months ago. Then I would have known better than to marry him. Not only is he a philandering pig, he can't pack a suitcase and he drinks cod liver oil on the sly. Yuk!"

She grabbed the handle of the suitcase and dragged it, bumping and thumping, off the porch to the dirt driveway, leaving a trail of socks and shorts in her wake. Then she went to her Mercedes and dug through the grocery bag on the passenger seat for the butane lighter she'd bought at the local convenience store especially for the ceremony she was about to perform. Printed in blue on the slim white case were the words: The more I know men, the better I like my dog. Setting fire to the edge of Ross's airline ticket for their honeymoon in France, Bronwynn let a malicious grin spread across her face. She dropped the burning paper into the suitcase and stood back to watch at least eight hundred dollars worth of men's wear go up in smoke.

"What the hell are you doing?"

Bronwynn stared at the man storming toward her out of the trees as if she'd never seen a man before. She certainly hadn't expected—or wanted—to see one there. He was good-looking, not that that impressed her in her present state of mind—much. Okay, she thought, so he was disgustingly cute in a harried, yuppie sort of way. So what? So her mouth had gone dry at the sight of him. It wasn't attraction, it couldn't be. How could she possibly be attracted to a total stranger after the day she'd had? No, it wasn't attraction that was making her palms sweat. It was either angst or the giant soft pretzel with jalepeño cheese she'd eaten at the New Hampshire-Vermont border.

All-American Businessman was the label that came

to her mind from her modeling days, when everyone's look had had a certain name and marketability. In tan dress slacks and a white shirt, he looked as if he'd just stepped out of his BMW after a long, hard day of corporate ladder climbing. His sleeves were rolled up past his elbows, and his tie had been yanked loose. Thick, tawny blond hair fell across his forehead, not quite carrying out its threat to be unruly as he bent and scooped up a couple of handfuls of dirt and threw them into the burning suitcase. He flipped the lid shut with the toe of his shoe and stood glaring down at her with eyes the color of good Irish whiskey.

"What are you trying to do, start a forest fire?" he asked in a hoarse, incredibly sexy baritone voice.

Bronwynn looked down at Ross's smoldering Gucci suitcase. She'd been planning this little piece of revenge for hours, envisioning it again and again as she'd sped northwest on the freeway. Now this overgrown eagle scout had ruined it. Handsome or not, she was furious with him.

"How dare you," she said, her anger ready to boil over inside her like a pot on a hot stove. She flicked her Bic at him. "Get away from me. Get out of here you—you—you *man!*" She spat the word out as if it was the dirtiest thing she could think to call him.

Wade snatched the lighter away from her before she could accidentally set her veil on fire. "Give me that. What are you, lady, some kind of kook? Where's your husband? I'm sure he won't appreciate your setting the luggage on fire."

Bronwynn stepped back from him, her patrician nose in the air. "I don't have a husband. I gave him away at the wedding along with the bouquet."

Hands planted on his lean hips, Wade studied her a moment as she gazed off toward the woods. The cap of her veil was askew, revealing a thick head of baby fine, brilliant red hair. Her face was delicate with high cheekbones and a sculpted jaw. Almond-shaped eyes and a full, sensuous mouth lent her a rather exotic look. The wedding gown she wore hugged a tall, slender, model's body. She was barefoot. Her toenails were painted pink and had little red roses on them.

She was breathtaking, the way a purple orchid would be in a field of dandelions. Still Wade told himself he had no business letting her unusual beauty affect him. He wasn't the kind of man to stick his nose into a hornet's nest for no good reason.

Tucker wandered up, woofed tiredly at the smoking suitcase, and plopped down at his master's feet to rest.

Abruptly Bronwynn turned and marched back to her car without a word to the man who had so rudely interrupted her fun. Her anger suddenly had been extinguished. The flame inside her had turned to a lump of ice, and she felt oddly detached. Maybe this was what it was like to lose your mind, she thought. Guilt assailed her at the notion that she had survived the deaths of her parents but would lose her marbles over Ross Hilliard. That would have been a huge insult to her parents, whom she had loved with all her heart. Ross Hilliard was no more worth the trouble than the lowliest worm beneath the earth.

She pulled the bag of groceries up into her arms and marched up the steps into the house. Wade watched her go, annoyed that she had simply walked away from him as if he were a servant she had dismissed. His gaze ran admiringly over the red Mercedes 450SL. He wondered if it belonged to the missing groom. What had she meant when she'd said she had given him away at the wedding? he wondered. Running around barefoot in a wedding gown, setting suitcases on fire— the woman obviously was dangerously unbalanced.

"Who are you?" he asked, stepping inside the open

front door. She was standing in the middle of the parlor looking at the moldy cabbage-rose wallpaper that was peeling off the walls in rippling sheets.

Her right eyebrow arched higher as she stared at him. "Bronwynn Prescott Pierson," she said as if he should have recognized her. "Who are you?"

"Wade Grayson," he said slowly as his sharp mind called up the information he had stored to go along with the name she had given him.

Bronwynn Prescott Pierson. He should have recognized her, he realized. He'd seen her picture in enough magazines and newspaper society columns. The wedding dress had thrown him. Bronwynn Prescott Pierson, an heiress to the Pierson Chewing Gum fortune, model, jet-setter. He didn't know her, but he knew of her, and he'd had plenty of firsthand experience with her type. She was a shallow, spoiled, rich bitch who bought whatever took her fancy and flew to France for lunch on a whim. She was the last kind of woman he wanted anything to do with, but curiosity kept him from walking out the door. What was she doing in a dumpy house in the backwoods of Vermont, wearing a wedding dress?

"I'm staying at the house up the road for a few weeks," he said, inviting her to offer similar information.

"How nice for you. Enjoy your stay," Bronwynn said politely, dismissing him again. For now, she couldn't let herself think about having this all-American hunk as the nearest living soul within miles.

She wrapped her arms around herself, feeling cold from the inside out. She began to shake. How had she let Ross Hilliard fool her so? she wondered, wandering to stare out the dirty front window. Wade Grayson's big yellow dog had found one of Ross's custom-made Italian loafers and was chewing on it as he rolled onto his back and stuck his paws in the air.

She almost had married Ross Hilliard. All her life she

had wanted to fall in love the way her parents had—madly, wonderfully, totally in love. She had wanted to love with her whole being, to cherish and be cherished. She had so much love inside her to give. Yet she almost had married Ross Hilliard, and she hadn't loved him any more than he had loved her. She had been fond of Ross, comfortable with Ross, but she hadn't loved him. When she had discovered him with Belinda, she had been stunned and angry, but she hadn't hurt the way she knew she would have had she truly loved him. What was the matter with her, making such a horrible mistake?

"What are you doing here?" Wade asked point-blank. He felt a little uneasy breaking into her thoughts. She seemed detached, as if she wasn't quite in touch with the real world.

"Why, I've come here to stay, of course."

He looked around them. The house was a shambles. It smelled of mice and mold. There was no electricity. He doubted the plumbing was in working order. Who knew what kind of wildlife had taken up residence. It was hardly the sort of place a woman like Bronwynn Prescott Pierson would stay. He couldn't picture her staying anyplace that didn't have a complete staff and Jacuzzis in every room. She looked too delicate, too fragile for anything less than elegance. "You're kidding."

She gave him a blank look over her shoulder and turned back to stare out again at the overgrown lawn, remembering how it had looked when she and Zane had played croquet there as little girls. It had been like a fairy-tale house to them, the woods beyond like an enchanted forest. Her heart twisted at the memory of all the imaginary princes that had rescued them from one dragon or another. There were no princes in her life today. And she felt like Alice tumbling down the long, black rabbit hole.

Wade gave a half laugh and ran a hand back through

his hair. "Lady, you can't be serious. You can't stay here."

"I most certainly can. This house belongs to me. My great-uncle Duncan willed it to me nineteen years ago." She had been twelve and thrilled with the prospect of owning this gingerbread castle, but then she had gotten older and her interests had turned in other directions. Until she'd sped away from the church earlier, she'd all but forgotten about the house.

"And it's been remarkably well kept up every since," Wade remarked dryly. He crossed the room to a Victorian sofa covered in water-stained burgundy velvet. The upholstery was ripped and someone or something had made off with a good deal of the stuffing. Dirty shreds of the stuff trailed out of the hole in the center of the seat. He gave it a little shove with his foot, and three mice catapulted themselves out of the couch and disappeared into a hole in the baseboard.

Brows dropping low over her exotic eyes, Bronwynn stomped across the room and gave Wade a shove. "Keep your feet off my furniture, you man. Were you born in a barn?"

Wade stepped back and scowled at her. "No. This is as close as I've come to being in a barn in a long time."

"How dare you say such a rude thing about my house!" she said. Somewhere in the dim reaches of her mind she knew it was an unreasonable thing to say. The house was a standing disaster area. For the moment, though, she preferred to see it as it had been, bright and pretty with its fancy old furniture, and Mrs. Foster, her uncle's housekeeper, serving little tea cakes on hand-painted china to Zane and Bronwynn and their dolls and teddy bears. Life had been so much better then. She'd had her parents and her dreams. Now she felt as if she had nothing.

She felt emotionally isolated. Even at the wedding, surrounded by hundreds of people, she had felt alone.

Zane, too, hadn't seemed close to her, though her sister had tried to penetrate the strange wall of confusion Bronwynn had felt encased by for the last two days.

It was a frightening way to feel. To distract herself from it, she tried to ignore the confusion and focus her fading anger on the man in front of her. "Who do you think you are, barging in here insulting my house and telling me what I can and can't do? Who died and made you king of Vermont?"

"I don't need this," Wade muttered, shaking his head. He'd been sent to Vermont for peace and quiet, not to argue with some goofy broad who probably didn't have sense enough to wear a hat in a hailstorm. "I'm leaving."

"Fine," Bronwynn said, running her hands up and down the slick, cool satin of her dress. A tremor of shivers shook her, then subsided. She tried to swallow the knot of fear that felt like a tennis ball lodged in her throat. "The last thing I want around tonight is a man," she mumbled.

Wade took a step back toward the door. *Go and don't come back till she's gone*, he told himself. One night alone in this rodent's paradise, and the little rich girl won't be able to drive her Mercedes back to Boston fast enough. His feet dragged reluctantly back another step. "I mean it. I'm going. You can stay here alone with the mice and whatever else might be living here."

"Fine." She stood there looking lost and pale and cold with her toes peeking out from under the dirty hem of her wedding dress.

"There's a perfectly nice motel in Shirley—and three inns. There's no light or heat in this house," he pointed out to her. She just stared at him in the fading light. Something in her look tugged at his heart.

Oh, no, Grayson, he told himself, get your fanny out of here and away from this silly, strange woman. Don't go turning into a marshmallow simply because she's got that kitten-up-a-tree look.

He pointed a warning finger at her and shook his head. "I'm not coming back."

"Good," she said, trying to ignore the panic that threatened to rise up in her throat.

Wade told his body to turn and leave, but it didn't. Dammit, he thought. There was an almost frightening haunted quality in her eyes. Her square jaw had begun to tremble. She was shaking all over. He had the impression that if he touched her or spoke too loudly, she would shatter into a million tiny bits like a piece of fine crystal.

He snarled a little under his breath. He was a practical, levelheaded person with a solid Midwestern upbringing. He didn't get involved with silly women like Bronwynn Prescott Pierson. It didn't matter that she was beautiful and, apparently, available. She was the last person he wanted to get tangled up with.

He would stay away from her—even if she did look as vulnerable as a lost fawn. When she left he could contact her lawyer about purchasing the property, but he wanted nothing to do with Bronwynn herself.

"I'm going now," he said, not moving an inch. As an added threat he threw in, "And I'm taking my dog with me."

Dropping a mutilated shoe on the floor, Tucker sat down in the doorway and leaned against the jamb.

Bronwynn barely took notice of either of them. She felt the darkness closing in on her and wished for the bright flame of anger that had burned inside her all afternoon. Anything would have been preferable to the cold emptiness that was threatening to swallow her whole. Her long, fine-boned hands were like ice when she pressed them to her cheeks.

Her life was a mess. She'd walked out on a wedding she never should have agreed to in the first place. She'd almost married a man she didn't love. What was the matter with her?

"Ah, hell," Wade said. He had lost the battle within himself and placed the blame on Bronwynn as if she had been begging him to stay instead of waiting for him to leave. "All right, I'll stay."

Not listening to him, she looked up with a tortured expression on her pretty face and whispered, "This would have been my wedding night."

Then the dam burst inside her and the tears began to flow, and without giving it a second thought, Wade took her into his arms and held her.

Two

She didn't cry like a socialite, Wade reflected, trying to distract himself from the automatic flash of male panic at the sight of a woman's tears. Hers were no delicate sniffles designed for just the right touch of dramatic effect, the kind that barely dampened a monogrammed, lace-edged linen hankie. She sobbed, and the sound was so full of pain and confusion and despair, Wade almost joined in.

Even as he held her close, stroking his hand over her crunchy, white tulle veil, he cursed himself for being embarrassingly softhearted. There was little room for such a trait in his professional life. On the job he was very much the hard-nosed politician—tough, business-like, a granite-willed rock of determination. Off the job it was all he could do to walk by a puppy in a pet-store window. He got choked up when an American won a medal at the Olympics or fell in the attempt on the speed-skating oval.

It wasn't a trait he liked other people to see. A man was a lot better off having people think he was formi-dable but compassionate than having them think he was made entirely of putty. So he blinked back the slight mistiness in his eyes and tried to think of what he should do with the woman who was leaning against him like a wilting rose, her tears soaking into his shirt.

He turned with Bronwynn in his arms and backed the two steps to the sofa, sitting down and pulling her onto his lap. The move wasn't going to win him any style points, but he doubted Bronwynn noticed. She was about as cooperative as a corpse, dragging her feet then falling onto him, never lifting her head from his shoulder. While she went on sobbing, he tried to arrange her into what looked like a comfortable position, bending her knees and tucking her wedding dress around her bare feet. Then he heaved a sigh and wrapped his arms around her again and wondered why it wasn't her wedding night.

She certainly was dressed for the occasion, and the luggage she'd been so set on destroying had been packed with a man's clothes. So where was the groom? Had he stood her up? Even if Bronwynn Prescott Pierson did seem to be a bit strange, the idea of her standing at the altar, lovely and hopeful, then distraught at the prospect of an errant groom, was enough to break his heart.

He held her a little tighter, his pulse jumping unexpectedly as he felt the soft round globe of her breast press into his chest. For so slender a woman, she wasn't without feminine curves. Of its own will his right hand slid down to the flare of her hip and settled there.

Bronwynn lifted her head and looked at Wade. She sniffled and hiccuped and tried to wipe away some of the moisture from her cheeks with the heel of her hand. She looked about ready to reveal some deep, painful secret to him. Fresh tears brimmed up in her eyes and her lower lip trembled as she cried, "I don't have a hankie!"

Wade had been holding his breath, waiting for her to

say something significant. His shoulders sagged. He leaned forward, reaching into his hip pocket only to find it empty. "I don't have one either."

He could just as well have told her it was the end of the world. Bronwynn dropped her head back to his shoulder and began sobbing all over again. Nothing was right. The man she had trusted, the man she almost had married had betrayed her. She had betrayed herself by almost marrying him when she should have known he wasn't the right one. The house she remembered as a dream castle had turned into the *Amityville Horror* house. And she was having a nervous breakdown while sitting on the lap of a man she didn't know from Adam, while he was reaching a hand under her dress.

"What are you doing?" Bronwynn yelled. She pushed herself away from Wade and tumbled to the floor with a thud as material ripped.

Wade gave her a look and handed her a large square of silk that had been part of her slip. "Finding you a hankie," he said.

"Oh." She gave him a sheepish smile. "Thank you."

Wade watched her dry her eyes and blow her nose. Outside it was almost dark and getting cold. Part of him was dying to know what she was doing there, but the more practical side of him said he was better off not knowing. The best thing for him to do was point her in the direction of the nearest motel, bid her adieu, and go home. His stomach was complaining bitterly that suppertime was at hand. He had planned on spending the evening doing paperwork and eating a Mexican dinner with a baseball game playing on the TV in the background.

"Just to set the record straight," he said, pushing himself to his feet and running a hand back through his dark blond hair, "I don't go around molesting bawling debutantes. My tastes run in another direction entirely."

"I'm sorry," Bronwynn said, struggling to her feet as her gown caught around her legs. "But how was I to know? I'm not very keen on men in general at the moment. You could be the next Ted Bundy for all I know. You could *be* Ted Bundy."

Her eyes widened as she stared at him, thinking for the first time of how isolated they were. Wouldn't that be the corker? she thought. Leaving one louse at the altar only to be done in by another in the wilds of Vermont. A day couldn't get much worse.

Wade rubbed a hand over his face. He'd had her pegged correctly from the start: She was certifiable. "Ted Bundy is on death row in Florida. I'm going home. Drive straight through Shirley; there's a motel out near the highway. It's not the Waldorf"—he glanced around the gloomy, run-down house—"but it isn't straight from the pages of Edgar Allan Poe either."

Bronwynn hung her head and looked at the crumpled piece of fabric in her hand. Wade Grayson had held her while she'd cried. He'd found her a hankie when that task had seemed like the most important thing in the world. And there she was insinuating that he could be a serial killer. She couldn't blame him for wanting to leave.

"Thank you," she said, "but I'm not leaving."

Wade was ready to live up to her imagination's image of him and strangle her. "Honey, in case you haven't noticed, there hasn't been electricity in this house since Roosevelt was president."

"Nixon," she corrected, going to the table where she had left her bag of groceries.

"What's that?"

"Nixon was president when Uncle Duncan passed away. I remember because Uncle despised Nixon as he despised all politicians."

Wade's perturbed look deepened into a bona fide scowl that went unnoticed by Bronwynn.

"He actually voted for Pat Paulsen," she said, digging through the bag. There was a candy bar in there somewhere, she was sure. "You know, the comedian from *The Smothers Brothers Comedy Hour*."

Wade watched her unpack a box of Twinkies, a bag of potato chips, chocolate chip cookies, orange soda, and string cheese. His stomach growled. In the doorway, Tucker raised his head and growled back.

"The point is," Wade said with a sigh, "there isn't any electricity, and unless you're planning on dragging that suitcase in here and lighting it up again, there isn't any heat. It gets cold up here at night."

"I realize all that," Bronwynn said calmly. She felt much better, much more in control now that she had had a good cry. "I planned for a few minor inconveniences." She hadn't planned on the house requiring a condemned sign, but she hadn't expected the utilities to be hooked up. "I stopped in Shirley and bought a camp stove and a sleeping bag."

That must have wowed them at the hardware store, Wade thought. The mental image of Bronwynn strolling into Hank's Hardware in a wedding dress and plunking down her gold credit card for a sleeping bag and a camp stove was almost enough to make him crack a smile. The fraternity of old men that hung out at Hank's would be buzzing about the event for months.

"You really mean to stay here—mice and mold and all?" he asked, simply unable to reconcile the idea with the image he had of Bronwynn Prescott Pierson and her ilk.

"I knew there was a Snickers bar in here!" she whispered triumphantly, pulling the thing from the bag. Clutching it in her hand, she looked up at Wade like a child who'd caught her first trout. "Yes, I really mean to stay here. I appreciate your concern, Mr. Grayson, but I want to be alone."

Planting his hands on his hips, Wade ground his teeth. Did she really expect him to walk away and leave her here in this dump? *That's what you ought to do, Grayson. It'll teach her a lesson.* In the back of his mind he could see his parents frowning at him. They had raised him to be a gentleman. He shook his head. "I can't let you stay here; it's probably not safe."

Bronwynn set her candy bar down. If it had been lighter in the room, Wade would have had no trouble recognizing her "I'm peeved" look. Of course, she thought, he was so hardheaded he probably wouldn't have taken heed anyway. "I've got a news flash for you: This is my house. I'm staying in it. I don't need your permission or approval. And, as I believe I pointed out earlier, the last thing I want around tonight is a man, so feel free to leave."

"Oh, fine!" He raised his hands in resignation. He'd tried to save the goofy woman and this was the thanks he got. He took a step closer to her so he could really look down at her, not counting on being stricken by how pretty she was in her unusual way. The subtle scent of her perfume drifted in the air and enticed him to lower his head toward her wide, sensuous mouth. Suddenly it seemed hard to get a good breath. He blamed it on the mustiness of the house.

His voice was as rough as steel wool when he spoke. "That's fine because—" He lost his train of thought and blinked hard to clear his head, then narrowed his eyes at Bronwynn. It was her fault he wanted to kiss her. He didn't normally go around wanting to kiss women who wouldn't use the sense God gave them to stay at a decent hotel. "Because I've got a lot better things to do than hang around here."

"I'm glad for you," she said, backing away from him. She didn't like the look in his eyes or what it was doing to her blood pressure. She had enough things to worry about without adding unexplainable attraction to a perfect stranger to the list. She gestured toward the door. "Why don't you go do them?"

"I will." He jammed his hands in his pockets only to pull one back out to point a finger at her. "And don't come crying to me when something big and hairy goes bump in the night."

Bronwynn sniffed indignantly. "The only big hairy thing that's going to go bump in the night is you when I throw you out of here. Leave me alone."

"With pleasure!" He turned on his heel and almost tripped over his dog, who still was sprawled in the doorway to the parlor. "Come on, Tucker. We know when we're not wanted."

Tucker didn't seem as sure about it as his master. As Wade stormed for the front door, the dog hung back, his nose sniffing the air for the scent of junk food. At a warning snarl from Wade he hung his head and slunk out.

Bronwynn dropped down on the couch with a sigh, pulled her veil off, and scratched her head. What a strange interlude. One minute they'd been fighting, then she'd been in his arms, then they'd been fighting again—fighting each other and a strange sort of attraction. All in the span of what, an hour? She hadn't gone through so many emotions in six months with Ross.

Ross. She shook her head and sighed again. There was so much she needed to sort out in her mind, and she had come to Vermont for that reason. When she had left the church, all she had been able to think of was getting away, away to someplace safe and quiet. Immediately her uncle's old house had come to mind, even though she hadn't thought of it in years.

Foxfire, Uncle Duncan had named it. The Retreat at

Foxfire, the society columnists had called it. They were a pretentious bunch. She wondered if they knew fox-fire was a light caused by fungal growths on rotting wood—Uncle Duncan had always gotten a kick out of wondering that, as if it were a private joke. Uncle Duncan had always been a little weird.

At any rate, the columnists were going to have plenty to say about the day's events. Too bad they hadn't gotten a picture of the look on Ross's face when she'd denounced him for the cad he was. She didn't envy Zane the task of fielding all the phone calls and facing all the questions, but her sister had told her not to worry when she'd called her from a phone booth at a rest stop in New Hampshire. Because she didn't want the people she loved to be worried sick about her, Bronwynn had called and told Zane where she was going. No one else except Zane's husband, Tom, would find out.

On second thought, she felt sorry for the busybodies who would be trying to get the details. Her older sister was fiercely protective of her family and friends. The scrap hounds would be going up against a tigress.

"And what are you up against, Bronwynn?" she asked herself.

Confusion, hurt. Hunger, she added as her stomach growled. Forcing herself to her feet, she wondered what Wade Grayson was having for supper.

"No way am I giving you one bite of these burritos."

Tucker perked his ears and tipped his head in a way that usually won him what he was after. Wade was a sucker for a pleading look.

"I know that look. Don't give me that look." Wade scowled as he settled himself in the corner of the sofa with his plate on his lap.

His doctor would have an attack of angina if he

could see the pile of burritos smothered in sour cream and salsa that Wade was about to eat. Mexican food was not part of the recommended diet for someone with a budding ulcer, but nothing went better with a ball game and paperwork, in Wade's opinion. He figured as long as he followed the spicy dish with an antacid chaser, he'd be okay. He needed one anyway after his encounter with Bronwynn. At his feet, Tucker sighed and whined, thumping his tail hopefully.

"Forget it. The last thing I need tonight is a dog with gas." Punching the volume button on the TV remote control, he tried to concentrate both on watching the start of the game and on reading a report on the homeless.

Two bites into his meal, his gaze wandered to the floor. The big yellow dog had his head planted firmly on his outstretched legs and his most poignantly sorrowful look riveted on Wade. Wade rolled his eyes as he cut a burrito in two, put half on a coaster, and offered it to his pet. "I should have gotten a cat. Cats don't stoop to begging."

Tucker scarfed down his treat, rolled onto his back wagging his tail, and belched.

Cats, Wade thought. Cats made him think of Bronwynn Pierson. If she were an animal, that was what she would be with her lithe build and almond-shaped eyes. She had the personality of a cat too—quirky, strange, independent. Emphasis on the strange.

He'd done the right thing, leaving her alone in the creepy old house. What better way to convince her she didn't belong up there than by letting her find out for herself? One night full of the calls of the wild, and she'd be blazing the trail back to Beacon Hill.

He wondered if she knew how to work a camp stove. Could a person get carbon monoxide poisoning from one of those things? Irrelevant, she'd never get the thing lit. He thought of her flicking that little butane lighter at him, almost setting her veil ablaze.

"She's a grown woman. If she can't manage a camp stove, it's none of my concern," he said as he watched the second batter ground out to third base.

"Wait till she figures out she can't use the bathroom," he said with a chuckle. He could almost see her making a trek out to the woods behind the house, trying to manage all those yards of white satin . . . and a bear sneaking up on her from behind and her making a frantic dash for the house and stubbing her bare toes on an exposed root, stumbling and falling on a snake, then picking herself up and running into some cooty old mountain man who would drag her off and hold her prisoner in his cabin. Wade dropped his fork on his plate as his stomach rolled over.

He snarled at himself and his wild imagination. "Mr. Worst-Case Scenario. You're as bad as she was with that ridiculous Ted Bundy business."

Even as he told himself he was being foolish, he could see the headline: Heiress Slain While Neighbor Sleeps.

Absently he set his plate on the coffee table and stood up to pace, digging a cigarette out of the pack in his shirt pocket. Tucker wasted no time helping himself to the rest of the burritos.

If he couldn't get Bronwynn to see reason, he was going to have to take matters into his own hands. He paused in his pacing to take a double swig of antacid. The woman clearly needed a keeper, and, for one night anyway, it would have to be he.

Bronwynn sat back on the couch, swallowed up in the enormous double sleeping bag she'd bought at the hardware store in Shirley. Shirley, Vermont, she reflected as she nibbled at a toasted marshmallow, should have been the name of a B-movie actress in the thirties. Still, it fit the town. It was the kind of town that looked as if it should have a person's name. The feel of the place was familiar, comfortably worn, like an old pair of slippers. If Shirley had been a person she would have been the kind of mom who wore housedresses and pink curlers and cooked tuna casserole on Fridays. Bronwynn was glad she had come.

She wasn't quite as glad about her decision to stay at the house. It had seemed like the thing to do earlier, when the prospect of checking into a hotel alone on her wedding night had been a distinctly distasteful option. Now that night had crashed down around her, cable TV at Motel 6 didn't sound so bad.

The thing was, she always had felt safe at Foxfire— and not just because she had been surrounded by people she loved there. There had been something about the house itself that was welcoming and comforting. She would probably have been feeling safe right now if not for Wade Grayson and his comments about creatures and big hairy things going bump in the night.

It hadn't occurred to her until after he'd left that she had explored only one room by the fading light of day, and had done so when she had hardly been in a rational state of mind. That left roughly fifteen rooms where anything could be hiding—or anyone. Deciding she had used up her daily supply of fortitude walking out on Ross, Bronwynn postponed the tour and set up camp in the parlor. She was too stubborn to give in to unseen fears and leave, but at the first sight of something big and hairy, she was going to be out the door and testing her car's zero-to-sixty capabilities in a flash.

It wasn't so bad, really, she thought, surveying her array of shiny new camping equipment. She had her camp stove and a kerosene heater. A lantern on the claw-footed oak table created an oasis of warm amber light in the room. A broken windowpane was providing adequate ventilation, so she didn't have to worry about being overcome by fumes.

She wondered what had ever become of the caretaker of the place. Surely someone had been hired to look after it when her uncle had died, but he obviously hadn't been doing his job for a few years. It made her sad to see the house in such a state of disrepair. It had been such a wonderful, happy house. Now it seemed old, lonely, and depressed.

"We can be depressed together tonight, house," she said, lifting a can of orange soda to her lips, soda she spilled down her front when she heard a car draw near the house. Immediately her heart and her active imagination went into overdrive.

She was in a secluded, abandoned old house. People probably came out there all the time to do things they didn't dare do anywhere else. The people in the car could be teenagers looking for a place to have a party, or lovers driving out for a secret tryst, or drug dealers meeting, or the town maniac bringing out his latest dead body to add to his collection in the attic.

She scrambled out of the sleeping bag, doused the light, and reached for the rest of her six-pack of soda. If only she hadn't left the hammer out in the yard, she thought as she tiptoed into the hall, her blood roaring in her ears.

Wade loaded himself down with the camping equipment he'd hauled up out of the basement of Dr. Jameson's house. In addition to a sleeping bag and a lantern, he carried a five-gallon jug of water and two pillows. A bag of peanut butter sandwiches was clenched between his teeth. He found his way up the steps by feeling with the toe of his shoe. The front door was closed. Since he couldn't call out and his hands were too busy, he reached out again with his foot to knock. The old door creaked back on its hinges. He stepped inside and was immediately struck over the head.

Bronwynn screamed as she brought the cans down, and Wade and all his gear went tumbling onto the floor. Then Tucker wandered in, walked on top of his master's prone body, and began licking the orange soda off the back of Wade's head.

"Oh, no!" Bronwynn dropped to her knees and tried to see Wade's face. He groaned and opened his eyes, wincing. "Are you all right?"

"Just peachy." He reached a hand up to swat at the dog licking his ear. Tucker climbed down and wandered away, grumbling in his throat.

Bronwynn dashed into the parlor and returned with her lantern. Wade was still sprawled facedown, moaning. He looked up, blinking at the light. There were two Bronwynns, both of them wearing a wedding gown with a navy blue pullover sweater and pair of alligator wing-tip shoes.

"Either I'm seeing double, or this is what's known as a living nightmare." He gingerly touched the back of his head. "You gave me a skull fracture. I think I'm bleeding."

She shined the light on the back of his head. "You're not bleeding. That's orange soda. I hit you with a six-pack—well, a five-pack, actually. I had taken one can out."

"Gee, thanks for holding back," he said dryly, sitting up, rubbing through his sticky, wet hair at the small goose eggs the cans had raised. He dragged one of the pillows he'd brought along across the floor and tucked it behind his head as he leaned back against the wall. "You have a real flare for entertaining, Bronwynn. I've never been greeted in quite that way before."

"I'm sorry," she apologized as she gathered up the gear he'd flung down the hall. Her soda cans had remained hooked together, but two were spewing soda like steam from an overheated radiator. She left them alone. "In a way, it's your own fault, you know."

"You Orange-Crush my skull and it's *my* fault?" He

gave an incredulous laugh and rolled his eyes, then moaned at the throbbing in his head.

"Yes. If you hadn't spouted off about this not being a safe place to stay, then I wouldn't have thought you might be an ax-wielding maniac, and I never would have hit you."

Wade pinched the bridge of his nose as his vision began to clear. "You know, I think I understood that. What a frightening prospect. I must have a concussion."

Bronwynn sat down on his rolled-up sleeping bag and stared at him with her elbows on her knees and her chin propped in her hand. "What are you doing here, Wade?"

"A question I asked myself—not for the first time today." How could she look so darn appealing in that ridiculous getup? Her makeup was gone, her mane of shoulder-length red hair looked like an unmade bed. The truly odd thing was she didn't seem to care. Most of the women he'd known from Bronwynn's side of the tracks wouldn't have let the maid see them in such a state.

"I thought you had so many better things to do." She studied him as he squirmed a little, looking annoyed and sheepish all at once. He qualified as a definite "cute" with his wholesome kind of all-American looks. Even with his stubborn chin and a scowl pulling his dark blond brows low over his eyes, his was a friendly face.

"Yeah, well . . ." He dug into his pocket for an antacid tablet. "I didn't want it on my conscience if you accidentally burned this place to the ground or got attacked by a bear or something."

Bronwynn smiled at him in genuine surprise. "You were worried about me. How sweet."

"I thought you needed a keeper," Wade said, pushing himself to his feet and pushing his attraction to Bronwynn a good arm's length away. "I was right."

She stuck her tongue out at him. They may have been in the Middle of Nowhere, Vermont, but he showed all the signs of being a stuffed shirt, corporate type. How was it then that she felt this stirring of desire for him? How could she feel desire for any man after what she'd been through with Ross?

Maybe it was *because* of what she'd been through with Ross, she realized. Maybe she was experiencing a natural human need to be comforted, to be desired by another person after what amounted to a rejection. Finding out her fiancé had wanted someone else, that she hadn't been enough for him, had to be considered rejection . . . of the worst kind.

One thing her attraction to Wade Grayson was telling her: She had made the right decision in not marrying Ross.

"That's a great outfit," he remarked dryly. "You're really getting your money's worth out of that dress."

Bronwynn glanced down and shrugged. "So it's not haute couture. I never did make it to France today anyway. I was going to change, but I couldn't get out of the darn thing. There are forty ridiculously tiny pearl buttons down the back. Only a contortionist could undo them without help."

She led the way into the parlor and settled back down on the couch, tucking her legs into her sleeping bag as she watched Wade move his gear in. He gave her a look that discouraged argument or discussion and said, "I'm staying here tonight."

Bronwynn nodded. After the scare he'd given her, she wasn't inclined to refuse. Even disagreeable company was better than waiting for some ghoul in a halloween mask to sneak up on her with a chain saw. She waved an arm at the ravaged packages of junk food beside her. "Help yourself to supper."

"I brought peanut butter sandwiches," he said, settling cross-legged on his sleeping bag on the floor and digging one slightly mushed sandwich out of the brown sack. "Want one?"

"Do they have bananas on them?" she asked hopefully.

Wade made a face. "Don't make me queasy on top of everything else, Bronwynn."

"Have you ever tried them with bananas?"

"I don't have to. I don't have to try calf's brains to know I wouldn't like them either."

She was right, he was a stuffed shirt. He probably favored plain vanilla ice cream and kept the foods on his plate from touching one another. She sat back and munched on a cookie. "You obviously have no sense of adventure."

Wade looked around them. "I'm spending the night in the Munster mansion with a pyromaniac in a wedding dress, and you say I have no sense of adventure? What do you want me to do, throw some cobras around on the floor to make it more exciting?"

Bronwynn looked up at the cracked plaster ceiling and heaved a sigh. "No, thanks. I've had all the excitement I can take for one day."

"Do I get an explanation?" Wade asked. He thought he deserved one, but he wasn't going to force the issue if it really upset her. He watched her while he waited for her answer. She ran her hands back through hair that shone like dark copper in the lantern light.

"I guess you deserve one," she said at length. "I walked out in the middle of my wedding today."

"You did what?" Maybe she was even more of a kook than he'd first guessed. He wondered if there were people somewhere searching for her.

"Two nights ago we had a prewedding dinner. My fiancé, Ross, and a number of my relatives were staying at the house. Later that night I decided I was going to surprise Ross, so I went into his room and hid in this big antique wardrobe. I left the door cracked open so I could see out. Then someone else snuck into the room—my cousin Belinda. Well, I'm ready to jump out and grab her by the throat, when in comes Ross and he's not at all surprised to see Belinda. It seems he'd been seeing Belinda and planned to go on seeing Belinda, and we all saw a lot more of Belinda before they retired to the bathroom for aquatic sports in the Jacuzzi."

"Brother," Wade muttered, wincing. That had to be one of life's nastier surprises. No wonder she'd been acting so crazy. He abandoned his sandwich and moved to sit on the sofa. He reached out and ran his hand over the top of hers where it rested on her slender thigh. "It must have hurt," he said quietly.

Her smile was rueful. "Not as much as it should have. I was angry. Mainly, I was confused. Here I was about to marry the man and, in a strange way, I almost didn't care that he was interested in someone else. I was mad simply because he'd played me for a fool.

"You see," she explained, "Ross and I have never had what you would call a passionate relationship. We were friends. He was there for me when I lost my parents last year."

The part that confused her most was that if she hadn't felt anything other than friendship for Ross, why had she agreed to marry him? And once she had become engaged to him, why hadn't she paid enough attention to see what kind of a creep he really was?

Since she didn't know the answers to those questions yet, she skipped them. "Anyway, I didn't know what to do. It was such a shock, I wandered around in a kind of daze which everyone mistook for prewedding jitters. I didn't snap out of it until it was almost too late. I actually almost went through with the wedding! Then, in the middle of everything, I denounced Ross and took off." She gave a little shrug. "And here I am."

All Wade could do was shake his head. He plucked a cookie out of the bag next to him and munched on it thoughtfully. Tucker wandered in, snatched up his master's half-eaten sandwich, flopped down on Wade's sleeping bag, and went to sleep.

"So," Bronwynn said in an exaggerated conversational tone, "what are you doing in Vermont, Wade?"

"R and R," he answered absently, still turning her incredible story over and over in his mind. "Job stress."

His voice had a hoarseness to it, a raspiness that spoke of too many cigarettes. It was a tremendously sexy quality Bronwynn hadn't paid much attention to before. As her body responded to it, she tried to latch on to a topic to distract herself. "Can I ask why you're wearing a necktie?"

Wade glanced down at his shirt front, at the strip of brown silk. *Man, you really do need a vacation,* he told himself. "Force of habit," he said.

What an odd pair they made, Bronwynn thought, a runaway socialite and a burned out corporate executive. He hadn't said he was a corporate executive, but it took no imagination at all to picture him in a basic black suit with a proper paisley silk tie knotted beneath his stubborn chin. He probably was the heartthrob of the secretarial pool, she thought, knowing instinctively he would scowl at her if she said so. What an odd sort of relationship they'd fallen into. It was like a pendulum, swinging back and forth between antagonism and a quiet understanding.

She rather liked it. Too much, she told herself.

"What are you going to do?" Wade asked with a genuinely curious look, a little worry line jetting up between his dark blond eyebrows.

"I came here to think," she said, gathering up the bags of junk food she'd dined on and setting them on the marble-topped end table next to the sofa. "I called my sister and told her not to expect me back until I get things sorted out. Right now I'm going to sleep, and I hope the mice don't decide they want their couch back."

They arranged their sleeping bags and turned down the lantern. Wade gave her a pillow and ordered Tucker out to the porch.

"I don't mind if he stays in the house," Bronwynn said, pulling off her shoes and crawling into her flannel-lined bed.

"I mind," Wade said, toeing off his loafers. "He ate a whole plate of burritos for supper."

"Oh. Well, good night." The pillow had his scent on it, she thought, burrowing her face deeper against it—a pleasant, clean, male scent. He must have taken it right off his own bed. The idea unfurled a velvety ribbon of awareness inside her.

"Night," Wade murmured, settling into the soft down bag.

Silence crept into the room with the stillness of night.

"Wade?" Bronwynn asked softly.

"Hmmm?"

"Thanks for coming back."

Three

Bronwynn was awake just before dawn. Soft gray light and a cool breeze spilled in through the broken front window. On the floor, not three feet away from the couch, a little mouse looked up at her, as startled as she was. It dropped the cookie crumb it had been breakfasting on and dashed away.

Wade was sprawled on his stomach, perpendicular to the foot of the sofa. He had left his sleeping bag unzipped, and the top flap was only half covering him. His right knee was drawn up to the side, the toe of his sock only a few inches from their pile of shoes. His white dress shirt had come untucked. At the highest point in the curve of his shirttail, a triangle of bare skin was visible above the waistband of his slacks. He looked cuddly with his hair disheveled and his long, thick eyelashes laying softly against his cheeks. He must have been a heart-stealing little boy, she thought.

Oh, no you don't, Bronwynn. You can't go falling for him. A: You've got to deal with what went wrong with Ross. B: You just met Wade Grayson. C: He's a stuffed shirt—albeit a stuffed shirt who's a secret sweetheart, but a stuffed shirt just the same.

The man was there for rest and relaxation, and he was wearing a necktie. That fact alone should have been enough to warn her away from him.

Her first priority had to be sorting out her life. For twenty-nine years her life had flowed in a strong current that simply had swept her along. The last two years, however, there had been rocks and rapids. Now she felt as though she'd been washed up on shore, battered and bruised. It was time to take a breather. She had to get her feet planted firmly on the ground and her head cleared before she could plunge back in.

Slowly she sat up and leaned back against the arm of the sofa, drawing her sleeping bag up around her, a look of wonder on her face. When was the last time she had needed to examine options before deciding on a course her life should take? Never, she realized.

Things simply had happened for her. Her modeling career had taken her straight from high school to high fashion. Just when she had been nearing a point where she would have had to decide to retire or fall from the ranks of the top cover girls to jobs for "older" models, her mother's illness had made the decision for her. After her mother had passed away— her father having died in a car accident only days before—Bronwynn had followed her mother's wishes and spent a year raising funds for the Cancer Society. Her wedding to Ross marked the end of that year.

What now?

A trip to the bathroom for starters. She had figured out there would be no running water without electricity, because the well had an electric pump. But there were four bathrooms in the house, and if they had been neglected the way the rest of the house had, they would still have water in them, therefore she could flush, she thought.

Wade cracked an eye open as Bronwynn tiptoed from the room. When she was gone, he rolled onto his back and stared up at the ceiling, yawning and rubbing a hand over the dark stubble of his morning beard. He wondered how long it would be before Bronwynn packed up her camp stove and headed for more luxurious accommodations. A couple of hours maybe—maybe less once she got a look at the bathroom; there was stuff growing in there scientists had yet to name.

He felt a little twinge of disappointment at the prospect of her leaving. It wasn't that he wanted to spend the day with her, he hastened to assure himself. He wanted her gone—ASAP. The sooner she was gone, the sooner he could put his plans in motion to buy the property and the sooner he could get down to the business of rest and relaxation. He certainly wasn't getting much of either since he'd met Bronwynn. Except he . . . he . . . kind of wanted to spend the day with her.

Uh-uh, Grayson. She's nothing but trouble. She beaned you with a six-pack, that should tell you something. So she gets your hormones dancing. There are plenty of women who can do that without giving you a worse ulcer than the one you've already got.

Off the top of his head he couldn't name one, but there were plenty, he was sure. Somewhere. The truth was, he hadn't been looking much lately. He'd been so consumed by his work, he hadn't had time for a social life. Obviously that was why he was finding himself attracted to Bronwynn. It had been a long time, and she certainly was pretty. He breathed a sigh of relief. Lust he understood. Lust could be controlled.

Part of what he was feeling for Bronwynn no doubt was sympathy and compassion. He couldn't begin to imagine what it would be like to make the kind of discovery she had made. But he could remember the pain and confusion that had filled her eyes right before she'd broken down, and the memory made him hurt all over.

What kind of jerk was this Ross character? The worst kind, Wade decided. The man hadn't even tried to redeem himself by coming after Bronwynn; he'd just let her go. Her methods may have been a little unorthodox, but Wade had to agree, she'd done the right thing in leaving the clown.

A reluctant smile spread across his face. If Bronwynn had put on half the show at the wedding that she had when setting Ross's luggage on fire, it would have been worth paying admission to have been there. No question, she had set Boston society on its ear. As he had seen for himself, life did not remain dull with Bronwynn around.

No sooner had he completed the thought when a scream split the air. Wade was on his feet and into the hall in a flash. A second scream directed him toward the back of the house. He ran down the long hall in his socks, glancing into each room as he went in search of Bronwynn. The bathroom door swung out just as he turned. He managed to dodge it, but stubbed his big toe in the process.

"Ouch! Dammit! You broke my toe!" He leaned back against the wall, holding his wounded foot, glaring at Bronwynn.

Bronwynn wasn't paying any attention to him. She looked as though she had just met the devil face-to-face. "Wade! Wade! It's a sn—sn—sn—"

"Snake?"

"Python!" She spat the word out, wiggling and shuddering.

"Python!" He rolled his eyes and headed back to the parlor, limping slightly, Bronwynn hot on his heels.

"It's huge and it went right over my foot! Yuk! Yuk, yuk, yuk!"

Wade sat down on the sofa and pulled his sock off, his brows knitting together as he carefully examined his toe.

"This is no time to be playing with your feet!" Bronwynn said in a snappy tone, sitting next to him, curling her own feet under her as she cast a wary glance at the floor. She dragged a hand back through her hair and shuddered again. "Not with Monty Python on the loose in my bathroom."

"Bronwynn," Wade said tiredly, "this is Vermont. There are no pythons in Vermont."

"Feel free to break the news to our legless friend in the bathroom, Mr. Science. You can explain it to him as you introduce him to the great outdoors."

He gave her a sideways look as he rubbed his toe. "Maybe you should let him stay. He'll help put a dent in the mouse population."

"I prefer exterminators, they walk upright." She stuck her left foot out and frowned at it. Like an idiot, she had left her shoes off. She hadn't wanted to disturb Wade's sleep by clomping around in her wing tips. Now a hideous creature had slithered over her skin. "And there's going to be a troop of them in here first thing Monday morning."

"You're staying?" he asked cautiously.

"I don't know how long I'm staying, but it doesn't matter. I can't have the place going to ruin like this," she said, picking at a tuft of stuffing coming through the arm of the sofa.

Pulling his sock back on, Wade forced a weak smile. "I thought you'd take one look at this place in the bright light of day and run straight to the nearest realtor."

"I've never given any thought to selling it," she said with a shrug. "Until yesterday, I'd practically forgotten it existed." A worried frown tugged at her eyebrows. "Did you really break your toe?"

He eased his shoe on. "No. It's just sore." He gave her a stern look. "You're hard on a man, Bronwynn. Has anyone ever told you that?"

"Maybe you're just accident-prone," she said.

"Right." Wade rolled his eyes. "I accidentally walked under that six-pack last night, and it accidentally gave me a concussion."

"I am sorry about that." She climbed off the couch and went to the table to open her box of Twinkies. She tossed two to Wade and brought him a can of orange soda. "The least I can do is offer you breakfast."

He made a silent apology to his doctor and dug in. For months he had been promising Dr. Jameson that he would start eating right, but it hadn't happened. There was always an early meeting preventing more than a cup of coffee for breakfast, a crisis in his office that ran over lunch, take-out burgers for supper at his desk while he poured over the latest reports for the Subcommittee on Conservation, Credit, and Rural Development.

He would start eating right just as soon as he got Bronwynn Prescott Pierson out of his hair. He had brought along the information on nutrition and proper diet a cute little dietician at the hospital had given him—one who had been so impressed by the title of congressman. He had met with her for over an hour, and not once had she tried to hit him over the head with anything. Funny he couldn't think of her name as he sat watching Bronwynn devour another Twinkie.

"You said you were up here because of job stress," she said, licking a fleck of cream filling from her finger. "What kind of job?"

"Congressman." He thought she'd grimaced. "I'm a representative from Indiana."

"Really?" It was worse than she had imagined. When it came to stuffed shirts, politicians headed the list. "Where in Indiana?"

"I'm from Lafayette."

"I was in Indiana once," she remarked, staring across the room at a sheet of wallpaper that was so full of ripples it looked three dimensional. "I got lost. You really ought to do something about putting up more road signs. Or is that what they meant by the slogan Wander Indiana?"

Wade gritted his teeth as he lit his first cigarette of the day. "You're from Boston, aren't you?"

"Yep."

"Taking time off from modeling to get married?"

"I retired from modeling two years ago." She wasn't offended that he hadn't missed seeing her picture in the magazines. It amazed her that he'd known what she had done for a living. It was her experience that politicians didn't read anything but the *Congressional Record* and their own popularity polls.

"Must be rough," he muttered, arching a brow. She couldn't have been much over thirty, and she was retired. Of course, he should have given her some credit for having worked at all. He knew plenty of wealthy young women who had never lifted a finger for anything more strenuous than a manicure.

Bronwynn bit her tongue on the words *pompous ass*. What would he know about making an honest living? He was in a profession where he could vote himself a pay raise. He could go on a fact-finding mission to Tahiti and charge it to the taxpayers. Her temper was simmering just enough to lift the lid on restraint. "So all those Georgetown cocktail parties got to be too much for you?"

Wade scowled. "Yeah, I wore out my tux so I thought I'd come up here and hide out until my tailor has the new one ready."

"Don't forget to have him put an extra can of starch in the shirt," she mumbled under her breath as she sipped at her orange soda.

"Actually, I don't have a lot of time for cocktail parties." One of his greatest pet peeves was the idea some
people had that politicians hung out in Washington for
the social life and nothing else. He wondered how many
nights Bronwynn Prescott Pierson had stayed up until
three-thirty agonizing over the wording of a bill or
trying to find a solution to the family-farm crisis. "I
take my job very seriously."

He took himself seriously too, she added silently. "So
did I," she said. *Let him see your life hasn't been all
champagne and roses either,* she thought. He obviously believed she was some kind of social parasite.
"Until my mother was diagnosed as having leukemia.
Somehow after that making the cover of *Vogue* just
didn't seem so important."

"I'm sorry," Wade said automatically, but with sincerity. Sometimes it was just too easy for him to believe
that people who had it easy never had to experience
pain or loss of anything more than a few dollars on a
bad day on Wall Street. He'd spent a lot of time with
farmers who had lost their heritage, with homeless
people who had nothing, but rich people couldn't buy
health or love.

"I retired to spend time with her and help her until
she passed away."

So, they'd reached the end of round one of sniping
for the morning, she thought as she got up and wandered to her suitcase to dig through it for something to
wear. If she had to cut the thing off with a knife, she
wasn't going to spend one more hour in her wedding
dress.

She could feel Wade watching her. What was he thinking now, that she was a poor little rich girl? The sooner
he left, the better, she told herself. How she could feel
the least attraction for him was a mystery more puz-
zling than Stonehenge. In spite of their moments of

odd friendship they didn't get along at all. They were as mismatched as two people could be—a socialite who disliked politicians and a politician who disliked socialites.

Well, he was bound to leave soon. Then she could get on with what she'd come up there for, examining her life and her options. She didn't need a politician around to help her. He'd probably want to set up a subcommittee or something. The way things worked in goverment, she'd probably be ready to collect social security before he came up with a solution.

Wade watched her toss evening gowns into one pile and expensive lingerie into another. It seemed like a good time for him to bow out. He would go back to the house and take his own advice to steer clear of her. It looked as though they were destined to step on each other's toes. His doctor had sent him up here to rest, not to aggravate things by bickering endlessly with a woman he had little respect for and who had no respect for him. It wasn't any of his business what she was going to do with her life, so there was no reason for him to hang around.

He pulled his shoes on, then pushed himself off the sofa and went down the hall to find Bronwynn's "python." He would get it out of her house, then he could leave with a clear conscience.

"It was a garter snake," he said, returning to the parlor.

Bronwynn looked up from her suitcase. "Are they poisonous?"

Wade shook his head, more in disbelief than to indicate the negative. "Poisonous snakes are virtually unknown in Vermont."

"Did you have to touch it?" She made a face at the thought.

"No, it had made friends with a toilet plunger. I

carried them out together. They parted company at the edge of the woods."

"I hope he doesn't decide to come back for a visit," she said, surveying the outfit she'd settled on with a critical eye. White silk slacks and an emerald green silk pullover blouse was definitely overdressing, but she'd packed for Versailles not Vermont. "Thanks for getting rid of him, Wade."

"Sure." He rolled up his sleeping bag and gathered his gear, trying to ignore his disappointment at the thought of leaving. He forced himself to remember every outrageous thing she'd said or done since he'd met her and steeled himself against the memory of her weeping in his arms.

"You're leaving," she said, cursing herself for feeling disappointed. He was irascible, but she had enjoyed sparring with him. Maybe she was turning into some kind of sadomasochist. She grimaced inwardly.

"Yeah. I've got a lot of things to do," he said, leaning back against the door jamb and ramming his hands in his pockets.

She refrained from pointing out to him that people who were on vacation for rest and relaxation didn't generally have lots of things to do. Instead she accepted the lame excuse without comment and told herself she was glad he was going.

"So," he said, not moving. "I'd better be going."

"Right." Bronwynn bit her lip and shot him a questioning glance. "Can I ask you one more small favor before you go?"

His eyes narrowed. "What?"

"I really can't get out of this dress. Could you undo these stupid little buttons?"

Wade froze for a moment as she stood and presented her back to him. She had peeled off the sweater she had worn during the night. Forty round pearl buttons ran in a line down her elegant back. Several on either end of the line had been slipped from their loops, but the majority held the back of the beaded white satin dress together, just waiting for him to free them. He swallowed hard.

What a perfect opportunity for you to show yourself you can control your lust, his conscience seemed to say. *You're not attracted to her beyond the physical sense. Obviously she's not attracted to you or she wouldn't be so nonchalant about asking you to un-button her dress. She was a model. Endless fashion shows and photography sessions have made her im-mune to having someone help her take off her clothes. The gesture should mean as little to you as it does to her.*

Then why were his palms sweating? he wondered.

She shot an expectant look at him over her shoulder as she lifted her fiery red hair out of the way.

Wade cleared his throat and pushed himself from the doorway. "Sure."

His fingers were shaking as he fumbled with the first tiny button. The tight loop relinquished its hold, and he moved on to the next one and the next. As buttons and loops went their separate ways, an ever widening vee of pale, creamy skin was exposed to Wade's gaze. She looked softer and smoother than the satin dress. From the nape of her neck, where baby fine curls were stirred by his breath, rose the alluring scent of her perfume, tempting him to lower his head.

Bronwynn tried to force her heart out of her throat. It hadn't occurred to her that her body would react to his touch. The feel of his fingers plucking open her dress was sending currents of electricity directly from her back to her breasts. The heat of his breath on the back of her neck poured down over her, melting her knees until it was all she could do to keep herself from falling back against him.

She had hesitated to ask the favor of Wade because she had thought it might embarrass a stuffed shirt like him, *not* because she had thought it would have any effect on her. Over the course of her career she had had dozens of people perform the same task, many of them strangers as Wade was.

Maybe that was the problem. He wasn't exactly a stranger, and she wasn't exactly immune. Just because her mind didn't want her to be attracted to him didn't mean her body would agree.

"There," he said in a hoarse rasp. "All done."

"Thanks," she said, turning to face him. "I really . . ."

The word trailed away into nothingness as she looked up at Wade. The expression in his eyes was almost fierce as he stared down at her. A muscle in his cheek twitched, betraying the fact that he was fighting an inner battle. When he leaned down and took her mouth with his, she wondered if he'd won or lost.

Lost, he thought as he moved his mouth angrily against hers at first. He'd lost the battle, then he was lost, lost in the kiss. Her mouth was generous with its secrets, as soft as rose petals, as sweet as forbidden candy. He drank in the sweetness, knowing instantly he could become addicted, but at the moment not able to say no.

Taken by surprise by Wade and her own desire, Bronwynn gave up without a fight. Her hands clutched at his upper arms as he pulled her against him and deepened the kiss. His hands slid into the open back of her dress and caressed her from shoulder to hip, setting fire to every nerve ending he came in contact with. Bronwynn pressed herself closer still, stunned and excited by the need that rocketed out of control at the feel of his hardness against her. She had never known anything like what she was feeling inside her. Nothing had ever been as all-consuming as the sensation that was taking her over.

Wade broke the kiss to trail his mouth down the slender column of her throat as he peeled one shoulder of her dress away from her skin. He was not a man ordinarily ruled by physical needs, but a sudden rampaging desire had trampled his logical mind. Need was the only thing he could think of now—the need to make love to Bronwynn, the need to hold her and comfort her, the need to ease the throbbing ache that pounded through his whole body and echoed back from hers.

The sound of a car coming up the drive forced them both back to reality. Reality was two people who couldn't have been more different, two people who were pretty certain they didn't even like each other. Reality was a congressman on a very temporary hiatus from the pressures of politics and a woman who needed to find herself before she could look for romance.

"That shouldn't have happened," Wade said, forcing himself to take a step back from her. He stared down into her eyes, realizing for the first time that one was blue and one was green. Somehow it didn't surprise him. "I'm sorry."

Bronwynn held her dress up at the throat with one hand, thinking reality wasn't much of a balm for wounded pride. He made it sound as though he'd kissed her against his will. He had. She knew he didn't think any more of her than she did of him. Why did that sting so?

She stuck her chin out. "Just so it doesn't happen again, because I'm swearing off men for at least a year."

"Is that so?" he asked. She could have acted a little bit as if she wanted it to happen again, he thought crossly.

"Yes, it is. In fact, I was thinking of taking up that motto: A woman needs a man like a fish needs a . . . sailboat."

"Bicycle," he corrected. "A woman needs a man like a fish needs a bicycle."

"Why would a fish need a bicycle?" she asked, annoyed at him for correcting her big proclamation as if he were some compulsive English teacher.

"It wouldn't!" he said, his hands as well as his voice expressing his aggravation. He'd had more weird conversations in the last fourteen hours than he'd had in his entire life. "That's the whole point! The saying is, a woman needs a man like a fish needs a bicycle."

Bronwynn sniffed at him. "Leave it to a politician to split hairs! A fish wouldn't need a sailboat either, and I can make up my own sayings if I want to."

"Write a whole book of them if you like. I couldn't care less."

"Fine."

"Great."

They went right on staring at each other when they heard the front door open, as if there was some magnetic force drawing whiskey brown eyes to one green and one blue, as if the first to look away would be admitting defeat.

A woman's voice called from the front hall. "Bronwynn? There's a big dog sitting behind the wheel of your car. Bronwynn, where are you?"

"In here, Zanie," Bronwynn called back, still not looking away from Wade.

"Zany?" he questioned, arching a straight brow. "Must be a relative."

"Bronwynn, I—" Zane Pierson Matthews stopped short as she came into the parlor, her gaze riveting on Bronwynn, who was standing holding the front of her dress up, glaring at Wade who wore a rumpled shirt and a day's growth of beard. "Bronwynn, what is going on here? Who is this person?"

She directed an angry stare at Wade, and he noticed

immediately that her eyes were the reverse of Bronwynn's.

"Who are you?" she demanded, going protectively to
her sister's side.

"Me?" He shot one last look at Bronwynn. "I was just
leaving."

Four

"Bronwynn, who was that?" Zane asked, turning to her younger sister with a look that was both curious and concerned.

Bronwynn listened to Wade's car driving out of her yard. How could he say the kiss they'd shared shouldn't have happened? Well, she thought, it shouldn't have, but he could have refrained from pointing out the obvious. The kiss had been dynamite. The kiss had been dangerous. He had no business going around kissing her socks off then telling her it shouldn't have happened as if it had been her fault. She was well rid of him. Really.

"Bronwynn?" Zane shook her sister's shoulder gently.

"Huh?" She jolted out of her trance. "Oh—that was Wade Grayson. He's staying at the next house down the road. He's a congressman from Indiana."

Zane's black eyebrows drew together in disbelief. "Congressman? He looks as though he lives in an old appliance box in some back alley."

"Zane, what a nasty thing to say. He's a perfectly handsome man if you go for the young Kennedy type. Of course he was a little rumpled looking; we did just get up—"

"Did just get up from where?" Zane's eyes appeared to have doubled in size. Her face was as white as chalk.

Bronwynn's mind was still half on the sizzling kiss she'd shared with Wade. "From sleeping. Where do you think?" Oblivious to her sister's distress, she dropped her wedding gown on the floor and began to dress.

Zane collapsed onto a medallion-backed chair, her hand pressed to her heart as if to keep it from leaping out of her chest. "He spent the night here? You spent the night with a man I wouldn't sit next to on the subway?"

"For heaven's sake, Zane, you aren't exactly Miss America first thing in the morning yourself. Give the man a break, will you?" She pulled the green silk top on over her head and shook her hair out, wondering briefly what she'd done with her hairbrush. Before she could dig through her suitcase for it, her sister grabbed her arm and dragged her to the sofa. "Zane!"

"Bronwynn, sit, *please.*" They both sat down, one on either side of the mouse hole. Zane's anxious gaze scanned every nuance of Bronwynn's expression.

"What?" Bronwynn asked. "You aren't going to start in on me now, are you? I deserve to look like hell after what I've been through."

Zane sat back with a little gasp, biting her perfectly painted lower lip and crushing the red silk bow at the throat of her blouse in a white-knuckled fist. "Oh, honey, what have you been through?"

Bronwynn shook her head. What was going on? She was the one who was supposed to be going over the edge, not Zane. Zane hadn't nearly married the bounder of Beacon Hill. She was certainly taking it hard, though, which really wasn't like Zane; she normally was a rock of stability. Maybe she was pregnant again.

Bronwynn pried her sister's fingers from the bow and looked deep into the green and blue eyes that mirrored her own. "Zanie, sweetheart, you're acting bonkers. Are you okay?"

Incredulous, Zane Matthews fell back on the sofa, coughing at the cloud of dust she raised. "I'm acting bonkers. You walk out in the middle of your wedding— not that I blame you—you run off to Vermont, you spend the night in a house that looks worse than anything Stephen King could dream up, with a vagrant who tells you he's a congressman, and *I'm* the one who's acting bonkers! Bronwynn, for heaven's sake, we've been worried sick about you! How am I supposed to act when I walk in here and find you with your clothes falling off you, and that man—" She closed her eyes and shuddered at the possibilities. "He might have been anyone, he might have been Ted Bundy!"

Bronwynn shook her head. "No, he's not. I asked him."

Zane was on the verge of hysteria. "What did he do to you? You can tell me. Then we'll—"

"Do to me?" she questioned, bewildered. "Wade didn't do anything to me." Except hold me while I cried and listen when I needed to talk and kiss me like no man ever has.

"I realize you could have been considered a consenting adult, but given your state of mind . . . I mean, I understand why you might have wanted to go to bed with a man after—"

It was Bronwynn's turn to look stunned. "Go to bed with—oh, dear—oh, no—Zane, Wade slept here, but not *with* me." Having cleared that little point up, she narrowed her eyes in offense. "Wow. Boy, what do you take me for? You think I'd just zip up to Vermont for a quickie with the first guy I ran into? Jeez, Zane!"

Zane ran slender bejeweled hands over her face as she breathed a sigh of mingled relief and frustration. "Of course that's not what I thought. It's just that after Ross—I mean . . . forget it. Can we start over? Let's pretend I walked in and sat down, and I didn't jump to the conclusion that you'd slept with that Wade person. Okay?"

"Okay." Unfortunately, because the thought had been planted in her head, Bronwynn couldn't seem to stop thinking about it. What would it have been like to have slept with Wade Grayson? She could remember enough from their encounters to piece together a scenario that was not unattractive. She knew what it felt like to be held by him, in passion and in compassion. He could be gentle and tender, but there had been a fiery demand in his kiss, a maleness that drew out the most basic feminine feelings from way down deep inside her. No man had ever made her feel quite the way he had.

"I guess I'm still a little off kilter from yesterday," she said softly. It was a statement that covered everything—Zane's concern and her own.

"It's no wonder." Zane's eyes misted over as she gave Bronwynn a sympathetic look. "Oh, baby, I'm so sorry about what happened."

"Well . . ." Bronwynn picked at a bit of stuffing from the mouse hole in the sofa. When she caught the gleam of bright little eyes looking up at her, she quickly grabbed a box off the end table and covered the hole. She smiled nervously at her sister, who was terrified of mice. "Twinkie, Zane?"

"No, thanks."

Bronwynn unwrapped the little sponge cake treat and took a bite, licking the cream from her lips as a thoughtful expression came over her face. She felt so much better today. Things seemed to be in the proper perspective. "I'm glad I didn't marry Ross. I have to consider myself lucky I found out about him when I did. The thing I regret most is the mess I made for you. Has it been horrible?"

A naughty smile lifted Zane's wide mouth. "Truth? It's been kind of fun, actually—aside from worrying about you. The paparazzi descended on Ross like flies on a goat, as Uncle Duncan used to say. Of course, there are some who think you ran off to be with another man. You win either way, as far as the press is concerned. Everyone has found out Ross is a two-timing snake, and the consensus is it would serve him right if you had run off with someone else."

"Uncle Duncan." Bronwynn leaned back, polishing off her Twinkie. "Isn't it funny? I hadn't thought about him in years. Now here we are in his house quoting him. I just realized I miss him. I missed this house."

Zane looked around at the dirt and the ruined furniture, the cracked plaster and the peeling wallpaper. "It's a shame the place went to pot this way. I can't believe you spent the night here." She shuddered as she stood up and went to lift Bronwynn's wedding gown off the grimy floor. "Well, let's get you packed and out of here."

"I'm not going back, Zane."

The briefest beat of silence expressed Zane's dissatisfaction, then she took a patient breath and said, "No, but we'll get you moved into a nice hotel, a place where you can relax and think things through."

"No, Zane," she said to Zane's backside as she watched her sister try to restore some order to the suitcase on the floor. She pushed herself to her feet and shoved her hands in the pockets of her silk slacks. "I'm staying here. I do need to think things through, get my life back on track, and decide what direction it's going to take." She gave a little shrug. "Might as well be doing something constructive while I'm at it. I'm going to fix this place up."

"That's fine, dear," Zane said. Bronwynn recognized the tone of voice as being the same one Zane used when her son told her he was going to ride his tricycle to Jupiter. "I came by a darling little inn on my way. We'll get you settled there. I'm sure the proprietors can tell you who to contact to make the necessary repairs."

Bronwynn rolled her eyes. No one seemed to think she was capable of taking care of herself. First Wade had told her she couldn't stay alone, now Zane. What these autocrats were going to have to realize was that she was an adult who had every right to make her own decisions, whether they agreed with her or not.

She *needed* to stay. For once she was going to take control of her life instead of allowing herself to simply be swept along. She liked the idea of restoring Foxfire to its former glory. She wanted to do as much of the work as she could with her own two hands. It would be wonderful therapy while she figured out where she wanted to go from there.

And way, way in the back of her mind she was looking forward to having a certain irascible congressman for a neighbor.

"Express those reports up here ASAP, will you, Murph?" Wade took a long drag on his third cigarette of the morning. He looked out the picture window as an exterminator's van rumbled past.

"Wade, you're supposed to be taking it easy."

Wade blew a stream of smoke out on a long sigh and rubbed the back of his neck. He paced as far as the telephone cord would allow. Murphy Mitchell was his friend as well as his right-hand man. Murphy was one of the few people who couldn't be fooled by Wade's most charming tone of voice. He used it anyway. "So what's more relaxing than reading?"

"I can think of a few zillion things more relaxing than reading Brentworth's tome on paring down the defense budget—sleeping, soaking up the sun, making love with a beautiful woman, to name a few."

Bronwynn Pierson leaped to the forefront of Wade's mind. Damn, he thought. One simple kiss had knocked him for a loop. Why had he gone and done a stupid thing like kissing her anyway? He wasn't the kind of man who let passion rule his actions. He was a logical, practical man. The women he dated were logical, practical women. When they had sex, it was logical, practical sex.

So why was it when he got within an arm's length of Bronwynn Prescott Pierson, it was hormone happy hour? Even now his body tightened at the thought of her flaming hair and creamy skin, her exotic eyes and erotic mouth.

"Be discreet if you do meet a woman, by the way," Murphy added. "You know the press is rabid for sex scandals this year."

Wade stubbed out his cigarette, popped an antacid tablet in his mouth, and washed it down with cold coffee. "Yeah, right," he said, dismissing the topic. "I found out a little more about that piece of property we talked about. There might be a slight hitch in getting it. I . . . ran into the owner. She's reluctant to sell at the moment, but I'm sure she'll change her mind. Give it a week or so—"

"She?" Wade could almost hear Murphy's ears prick up. "She who?"

"Bronwynn Prescott Pierson. She inherited the place—"

His aide interrupted him with a string of highly inventive curses. "Bronwynn Prescott Pierson is there? You've been near enough to speak to her?"

He'd been near enough to do a lot more than speak to her, but he didn't tell Murphy. "Yeah, so?" With one hand he dug another cigarette out of the crumpled pack and lit it.

"So? The princess of the polo set ditches her fiancé at the altar and just happens to set up camp a mile down the road from the up-and-coming young congressman from Indiana. So? he asks me! Lord. This is what guys like me have nightmares about. It's the kind of thing that's making me go bald. Did anyone see you with her?"

"No. Cool out, will you, Murph? Jeez, you're paranoid. It's just a coincidence."

"Famous last words. Do you honestly think the press is going to swallow that?"

"Look, nobody knows she's here. She came up here to get her head straight—as if that were even a remote possibility," he added sardonically. "Nobody knows I'm here. Besides, it's not an election year, and it's not as if I've got a wife and kiddies waiting for me back home."

"Well, be careful for crying out loud. Maybe I am being paranoid, but you know as well as I do the reporters would have a field day. All they look for anymore is a guy with a healthy libido. It's like shooting fish in a barrel."

"It seems to me they're more interested in kinky libidos or adulterous ones," Wade said, tapping ash into a cut-crystal candy dish. He glanced at the little plaque on the coffee table that read Thank you for not smoking and flipped it facedown.

"Bronwynn Pierson is news, pal, with or without a libido."

Oh, she's got one all right, Wade thought as he remembered the way she had melted against him, the way her body had softened into his as he'd kissed her. Taking short angry puffs on his cigarette, he shoved the memory from his mind. "She's a pain in the butt is what she is. She's as far off the beam as she can get without actually falling on her head."

"Good. Glad to hear it," Murphy said. "Steer clear, and grow a beard while you're at it. Just in case."

"Jeez, Murphy."

"You can't be too careful. I'll talk to you later. So long."

Or too rich or too thin. Again he thought of Bronwynn as he hung up the phone. She was probably too rich. She was thin, but healthy looking, in spite of what appeared to be a ravenous appetite that fed on an endless supply of junk food. She had been a model, but she didn't look starved the way many models did.

Willowy—that was the word. Weird, yes. Too attractive. She wasn't beautiful in the conventional sense. She was exotic, and there was something magnetic about her.

Steer clear, Murphy had said. He intended to, though it wasn't because of his image. No. Wade had his own reasons for staying away from Bronwynn Prescott Pierson: She was goofy, she annoyed him, she made him feel things he didn't want to examine too closely.

He was thirty-seven. During the last fifteen years of his life he'd focused on building his political career. He was ambitious, yes. But he was dedicated, concerned, he wanted to make a difference. He was a patriot, and he didn't care if it was a fashionable word or not. Democracy fascinated him, both the straightforward principle of it and the endless labyrinth of the reality. The political world was his life almost to the exclusion of all else.

Wade couldn't say he had ever been in love with anything other than his job. He was, as Murphy had pointed out, a man with a healthy libido, and women were attracted to him. The few women he dated when he had time were career women, as wrapped up in their jobs as he was in his. They provided each other with intelligent company and mutually satisfying sex. His were always very discreet, very practical arrangements.

Very discreet, very practical arrangements that he was suddenly dissatisfied with.

And it was all Bronwynn Pierson's fault—somehow.

A plumber's van roared past, headed in the direction of Bronwynn's house. He laughed. He knew exactly what was going to happen. The house had taken her fancy for the moment. By Wednesday she was going to realize fixing it up was a dirty, messy job that couldn't be done overnight no matter how much money she spent, no matter how many people she hired. Then she would quit and go home. Something else would catch her interest, or some*one* else.

As he went to the kitchen to pour himself another cup of coffee, he wondered about the fiancé—Ross. They hadn't had a passionate relationship, Bronwynn had said. Lord, Wade shook his head, the guy must have had one foot in the grave. Just thinking about the way she had fit against him made his blood heat.

"So quit thinking about it, Grayson," he ordered himself, frowning at his coffee cup.

One of the great mysteries of the world, he thought, was how a man with a college education and a law degree couldn't manage to make a decent cup of coffee. The stuff he'd made could have stripped paint.

He looked at his dog, who was sitting on a chair at the kitchen table, obviously hoping to bum a Danish once Wade got them down from the top of the refrigerator. "If you could make coffee, you'd be worth something."

Tucker grumbled.

"I know I'm not supposed to drink it," Wade muttered, taking a seat across from the dog. "Who are you now, the surgeon general? I wonder if Bronwynn can make coffee. Oh, hell."

It had been forty-eight hours since he'd walked out of her house. He could have cut a chunk out of the national debt if he had a dollar for every time he'd thought of her since. It was so absurd. She was the last woman he would be attracted to, yet he seemed to be developing some kind of weird obsession with her.

He was going stir-crazy. The whole problem stemmed from this relaxation business. His vacation was ruining his temper. He got up as the front doorbell rang, ignoring the forlorn look Tucker cast him as the dog dropped his head to the table and sighed.

"Delivery for Pierson," the man said as Wade swung the door open. He was a small, bespectacled man with thinning brown hair and *Norm* embroidered in red above the pocket of his coveralls.

"Wrong house," Wade said, his gaze straying to the

white delivery truck parked in the driveway. The logo for Hank's Hardware was emblazoned on the side. "I'm Grayson not Pierson, Norm."

"I'm not Norm, Grayson." The man smiled pleasantly, revealing a space between his two front teeth. "Name's Wilson. Norm's having his gallstones out. Where's the Pierson place?"

"Up the road," Wade said, tilting his head in the direction of Bronwynn's house.

"Wanna ride along? I could use a hand unloading this stuff." Wilson pressed a hand to his back. "Sciatica."

Wade blinked at the man. Oh, what the hell? He was dying to know what was in the truck. He wouldn't admit to himself that he was also dying to see Bronwynn again.

There probably wasn't as much activity going on at a three-ring circus, Wade thought, although he couldn't remember the last time he'd been to a three-ring circus. A man on a tractor was mowing the knee-high lawn. There were people going in and out the front door of the house. In addition to the plumber's van, there was a phone company truck and an electrician's van parked in the driveway next to a rusted blue Ford pickup. It took him several minutes to pick Bronwynn out of the crowd, and when he did, he hardly could believe his eyes.

She didn't bear much resemblance to the magazine cover girl. Her face was streaked with dirt, her red hair was up in a haphazard ponytail. She wore a yellow T-shirt which was three sizes too big and faded denim cutoffs that made him choke.

Holy Mike, she had a pair of legs . . . they were long, long, *long*, and slim. They ended in a pair of sneakers that were so battered they were held together with adhesive tape.

As Wilson parked the truck, Bronwynn dropped the hedge clippers she'd been butchering a shrub with and came toward them. Right on her heels was a sheep with a blue velvet ribbon around its neck.

Bronwynn's heart skipped when she saw Wade climb out of the delivery truck. She blamed it on the canned spaghetti she'd had for breakfast. At the second little jump, she decided to give credit where it was due. Wade Grayson was a good-looking man. Anyone would have said so.

The morning breeze tossed his thick hair. The sun gilded the golden strands, emphasizing the darker hair that was streaked throughout. Bronwynn suddenly was struck with the wild urge to run her hands through it. She knew it would be silky and warm. The idea made her feel silky and warm.

Get a grip on it, Bronwynn, she told herself. What she was feeling was only a residual reaction from rejection. It was one of those Freudian things. It wasn't because she was truly attracted to Wade Grayson—even if he was incredibly good-looking and moved with sexy grace. He wasn't her type. All she had to do to know that was look at what he was wearing.

The man was supposed to be on vacation. Black linen trousers and a pin-striped dress shirt did not make the kind of outfit a person could wear to sprawl in a hammock or hike in the woods. His feet couldn't do much relaxing in wing-tip shoes.

"At least you're not wearing a tie," she said by way of a greeting.

Wade frowned at her. "Of course I'm not wearing a tie." He didn't mention he'd been reaching for one earlier that morning, but had caught himself before he had a chance to tie it. He felt naked without it.

Bronwynn brushed her bangs back out of her eyes and squinted. Above the noise of the tractor and the top forty music blasting out of a boom box on the porch she said, "I thought you were supposed to be resting and relaxing, not taking a summer job delivering for Hank's Hardware."

"It's a long story," he said, his gaze falling on the animal that stood beside Bronwynn staring up at him with curious brown eyes. "What is that?"

Bronwynn glanced down then gave Wade a look. "It's a sheep, Wade. You don't get out of the city much, do you?"

"I know it's a sheep," he said irritably. "Why is it following you around?"

Dropping down on her knees, Bronwynn stroked the animal's narrow black head and ran a hand back over the soft white wool, beaming at it like a proud mother at her new baby. "This is Muffin. She's the first pet I've had since I was a girl."

"You're a little out of touch then, Bronwynn. Most people get a dog or a cat."

"I'm not most people."

Wade arched a brow. "I've caught on to that fact already."

He looked around at the bustle of activity and gave his head a little shake. "You believe in diving right in, don't you? Are you sure you want to go to all this trouble? I mean, this old building may not be able to hold up much longer. Why sink a lot of money into it unnecessarily?"

"The house is structurally sound," Bronwynn said, standing and dusting her hands off on the seat of her ragged cutoffs. "I had a building inspector out yesterday."

She'd stopped him short. Wade wouldn't have given her credit for thinking of a building inspector, and it irked him. He usually didn't misjudge people, but Bronwynn kept throwing him curves. It would have been a lot easier to dismiss the attraction he felt for her if she had cooperated and been a ditzy bimbo.

The delivery man stepped between them and handed Bronwynn a clipboard and pen. "If you're Pierson, you can sign on line twelve. Come on, Grayson. We've got stuff to unload."

Bronwynn gave Wade a questioning look.

"Don't ask," he said with a chuckle.

He and Wilson unloaded a riding lawn mower, a microwave oven, a stepladder, various cleaning supplies, TV trays, four big fans, and three lamps. Bronwynn stood smiling at the foot of the porch steps with her hands on her hips and her sheep at her feet as she watched them carry things from the truck to the house. She felt so positive. It was wonderful.

"Gee, Wade," she said, handing him a can of orange soda as they watched Wilson drive away, "do you want to stick around until the furniture van gets here? You've got a strong back for a guy who sits around on his tush all day."

Wade scowled at her as he sat down on a step, fishing a cigarette out of his shirt pocket. "What a compliment."

Bronwynn held back a giggle. There was something about him that brought out the devil in her. She couldn't seem to resist teasing him. It probably was because he seemed to take himself so seriously. "I'm sure the delivery-man union wouldn't let you in. You overdress. What's the deal with you, Wade? Don't you own a pair of jeans?"

His gaze strayed from his neatly creased trousers to Bronwynn's long silky legs. The answer to the question escaped him. She had legs like a goddess, and she was swearing off men for a year. There had to be some kind of law against that. His mouth went dry at the thought of running his hands over those legs.

He forced his gaze to settle on her worn-out sneakers. "I see you ran right out to Goodwill and went on a shopping spree."

"Actually, I had my sister express me a few essentials," she said, unperturbed. "Cutoffs are a little more suitable for yard work than evening gowns."

Practicality wasn't their only virtue, Wade thought as his gaze strayed again.

With an effort, he turned his head and focused on the various vehicles parked in the driveway. "Whose junker truck?"

"Mine," Bronwynn said proudly, glad something had distracted him from staring at her legs. In another minute she might have gone nuts and attacked him.

"You traded your Mercedes for *that*?" The thought made his stomach churn even worse than usual. He'd always had a soft spot for a flashy car.

"Don't get a rash, Wade." Bronwynn chuckled at the look on his face. "I'm storing the car at a garage in Shirley until I can make space for it here. I thought a truck would be the ideal thing to have, considering the amount of stuff I'll be hauling around while I'm renovating the place. I picked that little beauty up for four hundred bucks. Isn't it great?"

Wade reserved comment. What could he have said? Not one woman of his acquaintance would have thought a rusting Ford pickup with half the front grille missing was great.

"I call it the Blue Bomb," she went on. "Muffin likes to ride in the back. Don't you, Muffin?"

Bronwynn glanced at her new pet just in time to see the sheep nip Wade's unlit cigarette out of his hand. She grabbed it away before the animal could devour it. "Muffin, you bad girl. I don't want you taking up a filthy, disgusting habit like smoking; it's bad for you."

She offered the cigarette back to Wade. He scowled at her and popped an antacid table.

Bronwynn was appalled. Was his stomach so screwed up he had to eat antacid tablets the way she normally ate butterscotch drops? She found the prospect oddly distressing. "Jeez, you chew those things as if they were candy."

Wade glanced at the roll of tablets before slipping them into his pants pocket. "Do I?" He shrugged. "Force of habit."

"Wearing neckties and munching on antacid. It's none of my business, but you've got some bizarre habits, Grayson."

"You're the one leading a sheep around," he pointed out. Muffin raised her head from grazing to stare at him in a most disconcerting way. "Where did you get this animal?"

"From Myron," she said with a sunny smile, waving to the middle-aged man on the tractor. As the latest tune from Def Leppard blasted out of the boom box behind them, Bronwynn's shoulders started moving with the beat.

"Myron," Wade said blankly.

"Yeah. He has the farm across the road from you." She gave him an incredulous look. "You've been here longer than I have and you haven't met Myron?"

"I don't think that's a capital offense," he said. "I've been busy."

Bronwynn probably had met everybody in Shirley by now, he thought sourly. She was one of those people that others gravitated toward naturally. Wade knew; he was one too—when he chose to be.

He couldn't believe she'd moved so fast to start fixing the place up. Truthfully, he had expected her to junk the idea and go back to Boston before making one inquiry about hiring help. She hadn't—that was another curve ball she'd thrown him. "Zanie went home, I take it."

Bronwynn nodded, absently pulling up tufts of grass and feeding them to her sheep. It hadn't been easy to convince her sister to leave, but she'd finally managed to get through to her. "She came to see if I was all right and to try to convince me to go home with her."

"Why didn't you?

She heaved a long-suffering sigh. "I don't know how many times I've explained this in the last three days. I intend to stay here and fix this place up. It's what I want to do. It's what I need to do. It's what I'm going to do. I may not have known why I was coming up here when I left my wedding Saturday, but I have given it considerable thought since I got here. I'm going to use my own two hands to strip wallpaper and sand floors. I may even try reupholstering some furniture."

"You're talking about a tremendous amount of work, Bronwynn." And a jump in the value of the property he wanted, he thought. "If I were you, I'd give it another long hard look before I found myself hip-deep in sawdust and tile grout."

Damn the man. He didn't think she was capable of doing the job. Even after what he'd seen today, he still thought she was some bubble-headed debutante who would run home crying the second she broke a fingernail. She glanced down at her hands. Three nails were broken and two were chipped, and she was damn proud of it.

"Well, you're not me," she said. "I'm fixing this place up whether you think I can do it or not."

"Fine," he said calmly. "But don't come crying to me when you've blown your trust fund on ceramic tile and then decided all this pastoral bliss is driving you crazy. You don't belong here, Bronwynn. You're a city girl. There are no posh nightclubs in Shirley, Vermont."

Outraged, Bronwynn stood up and sniffed at him. Wade pulled out a fresh cigarette and hung it negligently from his lip as he rose from the steps.

He wanted Bronwynn Pierson and her mile-long legs out of there, he reminded himself. The sooner the better—for both of them. They would both save money if she went back to Boston now. He was still certain she'd end up going back before the lawn needed mowing again. He was doing them both a favor by pointing out the facts. She could cut her losses now and keep the asking price on the place down where it belonged.

"You presumptuous, pompous ass," Bronwynn said, nearly nose to nose with him. "You don't know anything about me and I resent the image you've dreamed up. I've got some news for you, buster: I can do this job. I don't want your criticism, I don't want your approval, and—" She snatched the cigarette from his lip and thumped him on the chest with it in her fist. "I don't want you smoking in front of my sheep!"

"I shouldn't have taken his head off like that, Muffin."

Bronwynn sat cross-legged on her newly mown lawn, thinking about Wade. She and Myron had spent the afternoon raking. She had the blisters to show for it. The workmen had left for the day. She now had a telephone, some electricity, and one bathroom in working order, but both the plumber and the electrician would be returning.

Muffin grazed contentedly as the late afternoon peacefulness settled around them. Bronwynn tilted her head back and soaked up the sun. Tomorrow she would have freckles on her nose. A year ago she hadn't had the time to enjoy the sun or the heart to, having just lost her parents. When she'd been modeling, Mrs. Burns, head of the prestigious Burns Agency, had forbidden her to get freckles. Now she could have freckles if she chose to, and it was a good feeling—unlike the feeling she got when she thought of Wade.

It wasn't right of him to prejudge her, but on the other hand, what impression was he supposed to have of her? She came from a privileged background. Few people outside the profession realized what a tough job modeling could be. Her face was plastered all over the society pages in the papers. People who didn't know her thought she was a useless social butterfly. It might have been an unfair assessment, but it was a logical one—if the person making it happened to be cynical.

Wade Grayson was a lot of things. Cynical was one of them. Annoying was another. He also had the capacity to be very sweet. He'd done a lot for her for no other reason than he was a caring, considerate person under his abrasive, grouchy exterior.

She wanted to do something for him. She wanted to repay him and make a peace offering—not because she was interested in him, she hastened to add, but because they were going to be neighbors for a little while and because her instincts told her it was the right thing to do.

Bronwynn always went with her instincts. They had failed her where Ross was concerned, and she was going to have to figure out why, but she trusted them when it came to Wade.

She would give Wade a gift. She thought of him pacing around in his spiffy "I'm a congressman" outfit, choking from the tie he wore out of habit, chewing on antacid tablets, and chain smoking. Relaxation was what he needed. She wasn't quite sure how she could help him to relax, but she knew a good place to start.

With a look of determination, she hopped to her feet and started for her pickup. "Come on, Muffin. We're going shopping."

Five

The house was a little too modern for Bronwynn's taste. It seemed all glass and angles, but the cedar siding lent it a rustic quality that enabled it to fit in nicely with its surroundings. The name on the mailbox along the road read Dr. Jon Jameson. Must have been a friend, she decided, or perhaps Wade was involved in a time-sharing deal.

Taking a deep breath to muster enough strength, she cranked the steering wheel around and piloted the Blue Bomb into the driveway. Black smoke coughed out of the tailpipe as she killed the engine. Muffin stuck her head in the open back window and bleated a protest at the pollution.

"Sorry, Muff," Bronwynn said, scooping up the gift box from the seat beside her and sliding out of the pickup. When Bronwynn closed the door, a foot-long piece of chrome fell off the front end and clattered to the driveway. She shrugged and walked away.

In the open garage sat a black Lincoln Town Car. Bronwynn smiled to herself. The congressman might have coveted her German import, but he bought American. She wondered if his choice of a car was a per-

sonal preference or a political ploy. No matter, she told
herself, she was only there to repay Wade's kindness,
not analyze the man. The fact that she was going to get
to look at him again could have been considered a
bonus, but she didn't allow herself to think about
it—much.

A thought or two about his lean athletic body, about
his clean-cut good looks and thick tawny hair wasn't
going to hurt. What she had to avoid thinking about
was the mind-blowing way he kissed. She managed to
accomplish the feat once or twice an hour.

The front door was open, and she peered through
the screen as she waited for Wade to answer. There
was a neat stack of newspapers half a foot high on the
pine coffee table in the living room. News magazines
were piled beside it. She could see through the arch-
way into the dining room. A smoked glass table with a
marble pedestal base was nearly snowed under by a sea
of papers.

"Some vacation," Bronwynn muttered to herself, absently swatting a mosquito on her arm. She punched
the doorbell again and glanced around the yard. Wade's
dog was sprawled under a maple tree, dead to the
world. "Hey, Tucker, where's Wade? Where's your master, boy?"

The yellow Lab rolled onto his back and belched.

"You're not exactly Rin Tin Tin, are you?" Bronwynn
said, jabbing the doorbell again. He had to be there.
His car was there. His dog was there. The door was
standing open. As Muffin went to make friends with
the dog, Bronwynn let herself into the house. "Wade?
Wade, are you home?"

A groan came from somewhere to the left of the
dining room.

"Wade?" she called hesitantly, her wild imagination
running away with her. Wade was a congressman; he
probably knew tons of top secret stuff. Maybe he was

hiding out from spies or assassins. By the sound of his groan, they'd found him and tortured him mercilessly. Bronwynn's stomach knotted at the thought. "Wade? Are you alive?"

When he stepped into the doorway, Bronwynn went cold all over. He was as white and waxy looking as a piece of porcelain, making his dark eyes stand out in a face that was lean and drawn. His hair was disheveled and his shirttail hung out. He was barefoot. Propping himself up against the doorjamb, he pressed a hand gently to his stomach.

"Hi."

Bronwynn tossed her box onto the table and rushed toward him, her heart pounding. "Wade, what happened? What's wrong?"

"One too many cups of my coffee, I guess," he said, mustering a weak smile.

"You're sick?"

"As a dog," he said on a groan.

Bronwynn didn't feel very steady herself as some of the tension rushed out of her. "Thank heaven."

Wade scowled at her. "Personally, I'm not too thrilled with the situation. Turning my stomach inside out doesn't happen to be a favorite hobby of mine."

"Well, it beats being assassinated by Iranian terrorists."

"Debatable," he mumbled, standing patiently while Bronwynn reached a hand up to feel his forehead for a fever. Lunchtime had come and gone before he'd realized he hadn't put anything into his stomach all day accept acidic coffee and antacid tablets. By then his stomach had been ready to launch a full-scale revolt. No amount of pleading or promising from him could have prevented it.

"Dear heaven," Bronwynn said, worrying her lower lip with her teeth, "you look like death on the half shell."

"Thanks."

"Come on," she said resolutely, taking him by the arm and heading back into the hall, hoping she was going in the right direction.

"Where are you taking me?"

"To bed."

He followed her docilely, wondering if she would be able to drag him if his legs gave out; they felt about as strong as licorice whips.

"Gee," he said, his smoky voice little more than a growl in his throat. "I thought you were swearing off men for at least a year."

"This is no time for you to start getting frisky, mister." She led him into what obviously was the master bedroom, a spacious, masculine room done in shades of brown and tan. "Have you called a doctor?"

"Frisky?" he questioned, managing an anemic laugh that set off another round of mortar fire in his stomach. He doubled over and fell on the bed holding his stomach, moaning.

"Have you called a doctor?" Bronwynn demanded, her voice inching toward the unfamiliar edge of hysteria. Her hand was shaking as she reached for the phone on the nightstand. Damn the man. He was scaring her half to death. She was a lot happier with him when he was being pompous and insulting.

Wade managed to throw a hand over the phone before Bronwynn could pick it up. "I don't need a doctor. This isn't as bad as it looks."

"Oh yeah?" Her brows shot up. "That's what the headless horseman said."

"Really. I'll be all right." He motioned to a prescription bottle on the nightstand. "I've got medication. As soon as I think I can keep it down, I'll take some."

Bronwynn picked up the bottle and read the label. The physician's name was Dr. Jon Jameson, which explained a lot—so did the label on the pill bottle. "You have an ulcer."

Wade made a face as he eased himself up against the headboard. "Just a little one."

"That sounds a lot like being just a little bit pregnant." She set the bottle down and sat on the bed facing him, barely resisting the motherly urge to stroke his cheek. "Does this happen often? What set it off?" A look of pure horror fell over her face as a possibility struck her. "Oh my Lord. Moving that stuff at my house. All that lifting! Oh, Wade, I'm so sorry!"

"No, no, no," he assured her, automatically taking her hand in his to comfort her. "That had nothing to do with it. I got wrapped up in paperwork and forgot to eat, that's all."

"Forgot to eat," she repeated. To someone who ate almost constantly, forgetting to do so didn't seem like a possibility. She shook her head in disbelief. "Brother, you do need a vacation. Too bad you don't know how to take one."

"I'm on vacation," he said indignantly.

He was unbearably cute when he pouted, she noted. His lower lip jutted forward ever so slightly, his dark eyebrows lowered over his eyes. Now that he was lying down, some of the color had come back to his cheeks.

"If everyone took vacations like you, Disney World would go bankrupt," she said.

"To each his own," he commented tightly as he watched her disappear into the bathroom.

"His own what?" Bronwynn called out above the sound of running water.

Wade rolled his eyes and looked perturbed as she crossed the room and placed a cool washcloth on his forehead. "You'd be a real hit on *Wheel of Fortune.*"

"I'm shocked you even know what it is," she said sardonically, sitting down next to him again. "Your doctor yanked you off the fast track and packed you off to Vermont for your own good, didn't he?"

The stubborn, frustrated look he gave her told her all she needed to know.

Wade ground his teeth. He didn't want to talk about it. He viewed his ulcer as a personal weakness, something he had never been particularly tolerant of. He hated the way it was interfering with the performance of his job. He should have been back in Indiana now, meeting with local political leaders and the people who were paying him to represent them.

Bronwynn stood up. "Behave yourself while I go find us something to eat."

"Bronwynn," he protested, reaching for the pack of cigarettes on the nightstand. "I don't need looking after."

She plucked the package out of his grasp. "That's what you think."

"I don't need a keeper."

"Funny, I seem to remember saying the same thing." She shrugged, enjoying his disgruntled look, hoping it meant he was feeling better. "It didn't stop you."

"I suppose it won't stop you either."

"Darn right, Grayson." She sauntered toward the door. "Anything you can do, I can do . . . too."

"Better," he corrected.

She smiled. "Why, thank you, Wade."

Shaking his head, he leaned back and watched her exit the room, enjoying the view as much as he could under the circumstances. She had covered her breathtaking legs with a pair of jeans that were nearly white with age. They were threatening to develop a hole in the seat that hugged her sexy little, heart-shaped behind.

What a mass of contradictions she was. She wore old denim and designer silk with the same kind of careless ease. He'd seen her on the cover of *Vogue* painted up like a work of modern art. At present she wasn't wearing a scrap of makeup, and she seemed just as comfortable.

She was forcing him to completely revamp his ideas

about her. He didn't like it, but because he was a fair man, he would do it. He would do it, and for the moment, he would ignore the uneasy feeling that he was going to like his new impression of Bronwynn too much for his own good.

Bronwynn rummaged through the kitchen cupboards, excusing her snooping with the rationalization that she had to look in order to find something to feed the poor sick man. She defended herself by saying it would give her a better idea of who Wade Grayson was if she knew what kind of peanut butter he ate. She probably never would have agreed to marry Ross if she had snooped through his kitchen cupboards first. She could only imagine now the kinds of gross food he probably ate when no one was looking.

Everything in the kitchen seemed orderly. The freezer was stuffed with frozen Mexican dinners. She took one out for herself and popped it in the microwave. There was half a bottle of Chivas Regal sitting out on the counter.

Wade didn't strike her as a hard-drinking sort, but he definitely would be the kind to toss back a scotch or two in the evening to try to unwind. She wondered what Dr. Jameson would have to say about that.

In the cupboard with the tumblers was a jumbo bottle of aspirin and half a dozen bottles of antacid. At least there wasn't any cod liver oil. She found a can of cream of mushroom soup and put it on the stove to heat.

The paperwork strewn over the dining-room table looked to her like budgets of some kind. Bronwynn shuddered. No wonder he was sick, reading such intricate stuff. She got queasy just thinking about having to balance her checkbook. She easily could picture Wade hunched over the facts and figures, a cigarette burning in one hand, antacid tablets in the other. She looked down into the half-empty coffee cup. The coffee appeared strong enough to have dissolved the glaze off the china.

The man was riding himself hard into an early grave by the look of things. Bronwynn shook her head. If anybody needed a keeper, it was Wade Grayson.

She was the logical choice. The thought sent anticipatory shivers chasing over her. When she'd first seen how sick he was, it really had hit home: She cared about him—a lot. She hadn't known him very long, but they had been thrown together under unusual circumstances and their relationship seemed to have bypassed the awkward-strangers stage altogether. They were friends. It didn't matter that they couldn't agree on anything beyond the sun rising in the east. It didn't matter that they got under each other's skin. Wade had taken care of her when she had needed someone, she would do the same for him.

What made her nervous was that she felt more than just the pull of friendship when she looked at Wade Grayson. The attraction went much deeper—man-woman deep—and Bronwynn didn't think she was ready to deal with it. She might have known Wade well enough to want to help him, but she was pretty sure she didn't know him well enough to fall for him. How long had she known Ross Hilliard, she thought, and she had totally missed the mark judging him. She wasn't willing to take the same risk again so soon.

The easiest thing to do was to decide she had plenty of time to think about it, since Wade was sick as a dog. Never one to make a decision if she didn't have to, Bronwynn dropped the subject and carried their dinner into his bedroom on a tray.

Wade was sitting as she'd left him, but was now totally engrossed in the evening news. Bronwynn set the tray down, picked up the remote control, and changed the channel to MTV.

"Hey!"

She gave him a bland look as she pulled a chair next to the bed, sat down, and dug into her burritos. "If evil forces destroy the world while you're on vacation, nobody's going to come up here and blame you for it."

"But—" He started to protest further until he caught a glimpse of a scantily clad beauty in George Michael's latest video. Maybe he was in a rut watching CNN after all. "Wow. These things are kind of hot, aren't they?"

Bronwynn cast an absent glance at the television. What a basket case. He wore neckties on vacation and never watched MTV. She shook her head. "Yes, they're hot. So's your soup—for the moment. Eat up."

Dutifully he took a couple of spoonfuls of his bland dinner, relaxing as he felt the warm, creamy liquid coat his stomach in a way that soothed the burning. He munched on a cracker and stared wistfully at Bronwynn's dinner. The aroma of spices was almost as seductive as what was going on on the TV screen. "I could probably handle a bite of that."

Bronwynn licked hot sauce from the corner of her mouth and shot him a look. "In a pig's eye. It's no wonder you have an ulcer, the way you take care of yourself."

Wade rolled his eyes. "This from a woman who thinks Twinkies are a food group."

Bronwynn shrugged the comment off. "I don't have to eat right, I have a cast-iron stomach. But," she added, shaking her fork at him, "if my doctor told me I had an ulcer, I wouldn't pour hot sauce and scotch on it and set a match to it."

His scowl was directed at the television because he knew her remark was justified. He'd heard the same thing from Dr. Jameson more than once.

Bronwynn watched him thoughtfully as they ate. She caught herself wanting to erase the little worry line between his eyes with her finger. When they'd finished with their food, Bronwynn placed the tray on a table near the television set. "You know," she said softly as she walked back to the bed, "nobody would think you were a rotten person if you eased up a little and took decent care of yourself."

Wade set his jaw. He refused to believe he drove himself hard to get the approval of other people. He was dedicated to his job, to his beliefs. Admiration from others was part of being a congressman, but he could take it or leave it. He gave her a black look. "Did you come here for any reason other than to henpeck me, Bronwynn?"

Her bicolored eyes lit up. "As a matter of fact, I did."

She disappeared from the room, returning with a big white box adorned with a red bow.

"What's this?" he asked, suspiciously eyeing the box she placed on his lap.

"I think they'd better go back and check your SAT scores," she said, sitting anxiously on the edge of a chair. "First the sheep, now this. It's a present, Wade, a gift."

"You bought me a gift," he said in wonder. Boy, did he feel like a louse. He'd purposely picked on her, hoping to drive her away from the property he wanted, and now she'd brought him a gift. "Why?"

Bronwynn squirmed on her chair like a shy little girl. "Because . . . not counting your nasty disposition, you've been very sweet and very helpful. I felt bad this afternoon for having such a chip on my shoulder about Foxfire—that's the name of the house. Anyway, I wanted to repay you and apologize and say thanks."

As she chewed on her lip, her gaze locked on his. Wade's heart pounded against his ribs. She was so lovely and so sincere. Her sincerity was what struck him most about Bronwynn, he realized. That was the quality he hadn't been able to put his finger on. Even though she came from a world of wealth and power and privilege, she seemed untouched by it, innocent in some innate way. She was guileless. It made him feel like a slug.

She broke eye contact, clearing her throat nervously. For a wild instant there she'd been hoping he would kiss her again the way he had Sunday morning. And since they were in such a convenient location, one thing might lead to another and . . . She was fantasizing about sex with a sick person. What was she turning into?

"Aren't you going to open it?" she asked, breathless as she tried to push from her mind the image of lying tangled on the bed with Wade. "The box isn't the best part."

Wade pulled the lid off the box and burst into delighted laughter. "Jeans!"

"And a polo shirt and sneakers," she said as she watched him lift the stone-washed denims out of the box. "I hope the sizes are okay."

"They're perfect," Wade said, checking the labels. "You have a good eye."

Bronwynn shrugged. "A trick from my modeling days."

Of course, it helped that she had memorized every inch of his body. She'd practically gotten a hot flash in the store picturing him in the jeans and red knit shirt. She'd never had such a feeling when she'd gone shopping for Ross. "They're supposed to help you unwind. I don't think it's physically possible to relax in pressed linen."

Wade looked down at his crumpled trousers. He couldn't honestly remember the last time he'd put on a pair of jeans. Denim was hardly *de rigueur* on Capitol Hill. He'd almost forgotten the soft, comfortable feeling of a well-worn pair of jeans. Bronwynn had given that back to him. What a wonderful, thoughtful gift. It touched him in a way nothing else ever had.

She was damn pretty sitting there trying to gauge his reaction with hopeful, exotic eyes, nibbling on the corner of her wide mouth. He had to admit, she was unlike anyone he'd ever known. She was squirrelly, but she was sweet, and other than the fact that they were total opposites and had nothing in common, he couldn't think of a significant reason not to kiss her.

He reached a hand out to touch her cheek, his thumb tracing down the soft hollow beneath her high cheekbone. "Thank you very much."

Bronwynn blinked at him, stunned by the feelings his touch set off. He could just as well have reached out with both hands and cupped her breasts. The idea made the air seep out of her lungs.

Rein it in, Bronwynn. You're closer to the edge than you thought, an inner voice told her.

She meant to heed caution. She meant to scoot back on her chair when Wade leaned toward her. Instead she leaned forward and met his lips with her own. He threaded the fingers of one hand into the soft, fine hair at the nape of her neck, sending a shower of tingles down her back as he gently urged her lips apart. She braced a trembling hand against the headboard, a soft moan escaping her as Wade's tongue lazily explored her mouth.

When at last he ended the kiss, Bronwynn slumped back on her chair, convinced that she no longer had a single bone in her body; they had all dissolved, she was sure. A pleasant buzz filled her head. She knew if she was to stand up, she would drop like a stone.

Wade studied her reaction, amused and charmed. For someone who was swearing off men for a year, she didn't have much in the way of steely determination. Of course, he wasn't exactly proving to be a pillar of strength himself. He had vowed more than once to steer clear of her. Suddenly that didn't seem to be a very pressing need. The only need he was interested in was the need to take Bronwynn in his arms and kiss her some more. Touching her was like being plugged into an electric current. She made him feel alive and strong. She made him ache in places that weren't even remotely related to his ailing stomach.

"Thank you," he murmured again, his gaze never leaving her blushing face.

"Oooh . . you're . . . welcome." It seemed a huge effort to form the words and exhale them on a thready breath. Wow, Bronwynn thought, if he could bottle that kiss he'd have the world at his feet. The man should have had his lips insured with Lloyd's of London.

As her head began to clear, she shot him a speculative glance. "Aren't you going to say that shouldn't have happened?"

"I won't if you won't," he said cautiously.

What was that supposed to mean? She told herself she didn't want to know at the moment. She wasn't ready to make a decision about their relationship. All she wanted to concentrate on was her self-appointed role of overseer of Wade's vacation. Nervously she glanced at the enormous man's Rolex she wore strapped to her delicate wrist. "I'd better get going. Muffin will be anxious to get home."

"Muffin?"

Bronwynn nodded as she eased herself up on slightly wobbly legs. "She's out in the yard playing with Tucker."

Wade got up and followed her out of the room. "You left a sheep loose in Dr. Jameson's lawn?"

"Don't get your shorts in a knot, Wade. Think of it as a free mowing and fertilizing job." She stopped inside the screen door and glanced out. Her heart fell into her stomach.

Tucker and Muffin were covered with dirt. The dog sat in a newly dug hole, panting happily. The sheep stood munching on one of the many uprooted shrubs, basking in the glow of the setting sun.

Bronwynn could feel Wade standing behind her. Not because he was touching her, but because the anger was rolling off him in waves of heat. She bit her lip and stepped outside to get a better look at the damage, then she calculated the distance to her truck—just in case Wade flipped out.

"Perhaps I'll think of it as a freezer full of mutton," he said in a tightly controlled voice. He stepped down onto the lawn in his bare feet, his shirttail flapping in the pleasant evening breeze. Muffin abandoned the bushes in favor of nibbling at Wade's shirt. He yanked the fabric out of the sheep's reach, sending the animal a fierce look.

"Now don't go blaming this all on Muffin," Bronwynn said. Her pet trotted up to her to rub her head against Bronwynn's leg and stare up at her with adoring brown eyes. "I'm no expert, but I'm pretty sure sheep don't know how to dig holes. Dogs, on the other hand—"

Wade lifted a finger at her. "Don't even say it. Tucker is too lazy to instigate a disaster of this magnitude. The most diabolical thing he's ever come up with is getting into the garbage."

The dog dropped his head on his paws and adopted a look of innocent suffering.

Wade stood with his hands on his hips and scowled at the dirt-covered Labrador. "I know that look. You're as guilty as sin."

Bronwynn rubbed Muffin's head affectionately as she cast an accusatory look at the dog. "Corrupting an innocent sheep." She cleared her throat at Wade's expression. "Well, okay, they're both guilty."

Dr. Jameson's formerly immaculate, professionally landscaped lawn was a mess. It looked like the army reserve had conducted weekend war games on it. Wade raked a hand back through his hair. He shook his head. "Look at this mess. It'll take me all day tomorrow to clean this up."

Bronwynn had to bite the inside of her cheek to keep from smiling. She patted Muffin's head in a congratulatory manner. "Oh, no. All that fresh air and sunshine and physical exercise. You won't be able to ruin your eyesight or aggravate your ulcer poring over all the paperwork you never should have brought with you." She pressed her fingertips to her lips and gave Wade an apologetic look that was about as genuine as junk jewelry. "I apologize on Muffin's behalf."

Wade glared at her suspiciously. "You're enjoying this, aren't you?"

A little squeak escaped her as she pressed her fingers to her lips again in an effort to hold back her laughter. The brightness of her eyes was enough to give her away as she shook her head.

It would have been smarter to be angry with her, Wade told himself. He should have been angry with her, but he couldn't look at the sparkle in her mismatched eyes and feel anything other than a bubble of exasperated laughter. It wasn't like him.

She's a dangerous woman, he thought.

The warning went in one ear and out the other.

"I'll accept the apology on one condition," he said, crossing his arms over his chest.

"What?" Bronwynn asked suspiciously, stepping protectively in front of her sheep. "It doesn't involve mint jelly, does it?"

"No. It involves you driving that pretty little fanny of yours over here in that death trap of a pickup first thing tomorrow morning so you can clean up Lamb Chop's half of the mess."

"Absolutely." She grinned, her mind busy going over all the possibilities. He practically was inviting her to keep an eye on him. She'd keep his nose out of that ton of paperwork or die trying.

"In the meantime," Wade continued, frowning at Muffin, "take that beast out of here before I decide to make a shearling coat out of her."

"No problem. Come on, Muffin, into the truck. We're on our way home."

The sheep hopped into the back of the pickup. Bronwynn picked up the piece of chrome trim that had fallen onto the driveway and tossed it in the cab as she climbed in behind the wheel. "Don't worry about us, Wade. Out of sight, out of . . . your hair."

"Mind," he said under his breath, knowing it wouldn't do any good to correct her. The old saying was a crock anyway—at least where Bronwynn Prescott Pierson was concerned.

She may have gone out of sight as her truck's taillights disappeared into the dark of the woods, but, dammit, he thought, she was never very far from his mind. Even now the latest kiss they'd shared was replaying in his mind. Hot. Sweet. They had at least one thing in common—mutual attraction. As it became stronger, their differences faded into the background.

As the sun dropped over the ridge in the west, Wade stood with his hands in his pockets and a speculative gleam in his eyes, his gaze fixed on the thicket of trees that hid Foxfire from view. "Swearing off men for a year, Bronwynn? We'll see about that."

Six

"I know it's only been a matter of days, but Ross seems like ancient history to me. I think it's a sign that he and I were never meant to be. So I shouldn't feel any qualms about getting on with my life, should I? I mean, it's not as if I'm a widow and have to observe a decent period of mourning. And it's certainly not as if I'm going to reconsider, forgive Ross, and take him back. The creep hasn't even bothered to try to find me. He and Belinda are probably off sulking over the fact that they'll never get their hands on my money." Bronwynn paused to eat another handful of dry Frosted Flakes from the box. Stretching her long legs down the porch steps, she washed the cereal down with a gulp of orange soda, congratulating herself on buying the kind that was ten percent real juice.

Muffin looked up from her bowl of cereal to add her two cents to the conversation with a long bleat.

"You got that right. I'll bet they're in Mexico. I hope so." A nasty smile lifted her wide mouth. "Ross will get a heat rash. A heat rash *and* dysentery. That's mean of me," she reflected, then shrugged. "I don't care."

She leaned back and looked out on the gorgeous

morning, her freshly cut lawn, the lush forest beyond it, the worn edges of the Green Mountains in the near distance. The early morning air was fresh and cool and filled with the songs of woodland birds—thrush, finches, blue jays.

An incredible sense of peace enfolded Bronwynn in its arms and hugged her until every inch of her skin felt warm and tingling. Freedom. She had her whole life ahead of her and the freedom to choose any path she wanted, which brought her back to thoughts of Wade.

She wanted Wade Grayson and it had nothing to do with feeling rejected by her former fiancé. She had used her situation as a logical and convenient excuse, but she could see now it was a load of meadow muffins. What she felt was plain old-fashioned lust with a good measure of liking and caring thrown in.

It scared her a little bit. She had been so freshly hurt by a man, it was hard not to be a little gun-shy. If only she could have figured out what had gone wrong with Ross, she'd have felt a lot better about getting involved with Wade.

"It's not that I'm confusing Wade with Ross," she said to her sheep, who had scaled the steps and was nibbling at the flap on the cereal box Bronwynn dug her hand into. "That's not it at all. Wade just smacks of integrity. He likes to play the cynic, but I'd bet anything he never would betray a friend or callously use an innocent person for his own ends. Not Wade. Not in a million years."

Muffin took advantage of the faraway look in her mistress's eye, grabbing hold of the cereal box and bounding off the steps with it. She dashed around the yard with Bronwynn hot on her heels, running just fast enough so Bronwynn couldn't catch her. Finally she sailed up into the bed of the pickup with the box still clenched between her teeth and a triumphant gleam in her eye.

Bronwynn leaned against the crushed-in bumper of the truck to catch her breath, rubbing Muffin's ear with one hand. "We did all that running just because you wanted to take a ride in the truck? Well, we're going for a ride all right, but I don't think you're going to like it. I'll have to tie you up when we get to Wade's."

She scooted onto the bed of the truck, wondering what had ever become of the tailgate. "I know you and Wade haven't exactly hit it off, but he's a good guy, Muffin. He's got a lot of potential as a human being—if we can manage to keep him from killing himself with work and bad habits. I know he's a stuffed shirt, but you and I are going to do our level best to unstuff him."

They drove into Shirley first, to the nursery, where Muffin was confined to the truck, tethered to the spare tire while Bronwynn did her shopping. The geraniums and ferns she bought to decorate her front porch went into the cab, out of the sheep's reach. Planters and potting soil and garden tools went into the back. Muffin inspected each item, testing each with her teeth to see if they had snack potential. After several more stops in town, they headed out to the country again on the gravel road that led to Wade's house and eventually to Foxfire.

Wade was out in the yard when they got there. Dressed in the jeans and red polo shirt Bronwynn had given him, he was the picture of the man of leisure. Bronwynn almost ran the truck off the edge of the driveway when she saw him. The only thing that saved her from swooning was his lack of a tan. If he'd been bronze under that snug red shirt, she'd have been a goner.

The polo shirt showed off the width of his shoulders and hugged his lean middle. The jeans showed off other parts of his anatomy in a way dress pants never could. Bronwynn thought women everywhere should offer up a prayer of thanks to the makers of men's jeans.

Wade paused with his foot on the blade of the shovel as he watched Bronwynn unload her sheep. She lugged the spare tire out of the truck, tossed it in the grassy, shaded ditch, and tied Muffin to it with a long length of rope. She certainly had become attached to that four-legged ball of yarn in a hurry, he thought. He envisioned her walking into a swanky garden party with Muffin at her heels and had to laugh as he imagined what her upper-crust friends would have to say. It pleased him to think Bronwynn wouldn't give a fig about their opinions. Like her rattletrap pickup, she liked her sheep and wouldn't care who didn't.

A knot of desire tightened deep inside him as she crossed the lawn with a smile on her face. The morning sun turned her hair to flame, the breeze tossed it all around her head. Instead of reaching up to straighten it, she shoved her hands deep into the pockets of her baggy jeans. The faded purple T-shirt she wore bore the logo of an Irish pub in Boston. As she drew near he could see the pink tint the previous day's sun had put in her cheeks, the spray of freckles it had produced across the bridge of her nose. No woman had ever looked prettier to him than Bronwynn Prescott Pierson did at that moment as she stood squinting up at him.

On impulse—something so rare he didn't even recognize it—Wade dropped his head and brushed a kiss across her lips. It startled them both—the surprise of it and the burst of awareness it gave them. Wade recovered first.

"Good morning."

Bronwynn looked away, fighting to keep from giggling like a teenager. She was enormously pleased by his kiss, but she tried to tell herself it was because Wade was in a good mood, that he was relaxed, more relaxed than she'd ever seen him.

"Hi," she said, staring at the toe of her battered sneaker. "How are you feeling today?"

"Great." He discounted the slight gnawing in his stomach as being routine.

Over her rare burst of shyness, Bronwynn noted the healthy color in his cheeks. "Glad to hear it. Do you mind if we have breakfast before we start? I'm famished."

"From what I've seen, that's a perpetual state," Wade said dryly. He checked his watch, an action that did not go unnoticed. He had hoped they could get the lawn taken care of right away. The report on the defense budget would arrive soon, and he needed to dig into it. "I'm afraid I don't have much in the line of breakfast ingredients on hand."

"Don't worry. I did some shopping this morning. It'll be my treat," Bronwynn said, going back to her truck to get her grocery bags.

"Oh goody," Wade said, teasing her as he tried to peek into the sacks. "What do we get, cookies or chocolate cupcakes?"

"If you're going to get snippy, I'll eat both omelettes myself," she warned him in a prim tone, her freckled nose in the air as she marched to the house.

"Snippy?" he asked, out of habit reaching for the cigarettes in his shirt pocket, realizing there was no pocket on the shirt she'd given him.

"I happen to make an outstanding omelette." It was the only thing she knew how to make, but she wasn't going to spread that bit of news around. Part of her plan to help Wade included seeing to it that he ate properly. An herb and cheese omelette would have to do for starters, but she'd picked up a cookbook at the dime store in Shirley and fully intended to learn to cook a wide range of dishes.

Wade took a seat at the breakfast bar and watched as she stored her groceries away in his refrigerator. She had no intention of taking them home with her. She'd chosen fresh fruits and vegetables, lean meat, milk, all with Wade and his tender tummy in mind. She tried to look as proficient as possible as she brewed a pot of herbal tea.

"Do you know how to make a decent pot of coffee?" he asked, picking up half an English muffin she'd set in front of him.

"Nope," Bronwynn lied blithely. She poured two cups of tea and set one in front of Wade. "I prefer tea. Give it a try."

He made a face as he contemplated the tea, but he took a sip and decided it beat the heck out of the battery acid he brewed every morning. It actually had a pleasant, soothing quality to it. He was equally surprised by the quality of the omelette. It was light and tasty. He tried to remember the last time he'd had a decent breakfast but couldn't. It had no doubt been at a meeting, and he would have wolfed it down without tasting a bite. It was nice to sit and chat with Bronwynn and linger over the meal.

"Delicious," he said with a twinkle in his amber-flecked eyes. "Do you do windows?"

Bronwynn grinned. "As a matter of fact, I do, but you'll have to take a number and wait. I have thirty or forty to do at Foxfire this week."

"Why don't you hire someone to do them?" he asked, reaching for the cigarettes he thought he'd left on the counter. They were gone.

"Why should I?" She refilled their teacups. "I've got nothing but time on my hands. Besides, I'm looking forward to it."

"To washing windows?"

"And scrubbing floors and knocking down cobwebs. My first big project is going to be the kitchen." Her face was glowing with excitement.

"Figures," Wade mumbled, fighting a grin as she bounced a green grape off his head.

"I'm going to tear out the countertop and lay ceramic tile myself."

Wade shook his head in wonder. She was something. He didn't know many people—male or female—who would have been willing to tackle that monstrosity of a house alone. Bronwynn seemed determined to. He thought of the sketches he'd had done of the ski lodge he wanted to build and felt a pang of regret. "You really are going to tear into the old house and set it to rights, aren't you?"

"I am." She watched him carefully for signs of skepticism. None came. "Oh, Wade, you should have seen it when it was in its glory. It was so beautiful, elegant, but it was also warm and charming. It was a real home. I want it to be one again."

The way she was looking at him, he would have promised her anything. She was full of wishing and hoping, like a little girl at Christmas. He felt his ski lodge slip a little further away from reality. "You love the old place, don't you?"

She thought of Uncle Duncan and her family and all the wonderful memories Foxfire had given her. "As much as a person can love a place."

They worked on the lawn the rest of the morning, repairing the damage their pets had done, while the perpetrators sprawled in the shade, watching. The sun climbed, but the breeze continued, keeping them from sweltering. Even so, Wade peeled off his shirt and tossed it on a lawn chair.

Bronwynn suddenly felt in dire need of a cold shower. She'd seen her share of male chests and Wade's was no disappointment. He wasn't heavily muscled, but he was in surprisingly good shape. She guessed it was simply his natural build, because she doubted he took the time to work out. Lean and lanky, there wasn't a spare ounce on him. A mat of curls a shade darker than the hair on his head carpeted his chest and trailed down his flat belly. Bronwynn found the color contrast with his tawny blond hair incredibly sexy.

To distract herself, she asked, "How's your stomach doing?" *It certainly looks okay.*

"Not too bad. Thanks to the breakfast and the soup last night, no doubt. Thank you."

She shrugged, looking down as she shoveled dirt around the base of a juniper shrub. "What are neighbors for?"

He was hoping this neighbor was going to do more than see to the needs of his troublesome stomach. Dawn had found him out on the patio, stretched out on a lounge chair, contemplating his growing attraction to Bronwynn Pierson. He had come to the conclusion that he liked her as a person in spite of her eccentricities. She made him crazy with all her quirks, but she was never dull. In fact, she was one of the most genuine people he'd ever met; nothing about Bronwynn was an act. And she was one sexy lady, he thought, eyeing her pretty little backside as she bent to roll up her pant legs.

In his typically logical, analytical way, Wade had decided there was no reason he and Bronwynn shouldn't explore the mutual desire he'd tasted in their kisses. There was no reason except that she recently had had her heart broken.

It seemed like much more than just a matter of days since he'd held her in his arms and comforted her while she cried over her fiancé's betrayal. She had been an emotional wreck. Was she still feeling the hurt? Did she still harbor any love for the man who had deceived her?

She seemed to have gotten herself back on track. She seemed to have put the disaster behind her. Diving into work at Foxfire seemed like a positive sign to Wade. He had to think she'd been telling the truth to herself and to him when she'd said she hadn't truly loved Ross Hilliard. But was she ready to try another relationship?

Wade had decided he wanted Bronwynn in his life—and in his bed—but he wouldn't take advantage of a vulnerable woman.

They sat down on the shaded patio to rest when the last of the shrubs was in place. Wade pulled his shirt back on. Bronwynn served milk and deli sandwiches she'd picked up in Shirley. Tucker sat at their feet pleading for a handout with his big brown eyes while Muffin stood under the maple tree staring at them, bleating her heart out.

"Poor Muffin," Bronwynn said sadly.

"Poor Muffin," Wade repeated. "Mutton stew on the hoof."

"Wade!" she wailed, tossing a potato chip at him. He laughed and tweaked her nose. "You're a horrible tease."

"Poor Bronwynn," he said, chuckling. He leaned back in his chair and lit a cigarette, one of the last in a pack he could have sworn had been nearly full. Exhaling a stream of smoke, he studied Bronwynn through narrowed eyes.

She glanced around her nervously. "What?"

"How are you?" he asked, suddenly very serious.

There was no need for him to expand on the question, Bronwynn knew exactly what he meant. The odd thing was she didn't wonder how it was they were so in tune. It felt natural. She took a deep breath, carefully considering her answer instead of tossing off the usual "I'm fine." Finally she met his gaze and said, "I'm good. I don't have all the answers yet, but I don't have any regrets. I did the right thing."

"What are the questions you don't have the answers to?"

She made a frustrated face, propped her elbow on the glass-topped table, and leaned her chin on her hand. It never occurred to her not to be totally open with Wade. "I don't understand how I could have become engaged to Ross. I knew it wasn't the real thing. In my heart I knew. You'd understand if you'd ever met my parents. They had such a wonderful love. They really cared for each other as human beings. They were friends, but they had an incredible passion for each other too."

"It must have hurt a lot to lose them."

Tears sprang to her eyes. She didn't try to hide them. "I know I couldn't live through anything worse. We knew Mama was going. About the time the doctors had given her only a couple of months, Daddy was killed in a car accident. So sudden, so—" She paused and bit her lip. She still felt cheated when she thought about it. There had been no time for good-byes. "Mama died two days later. When we told her about Daddy she just let go."

Wade reached across the table and slipped his hand over hers, giving her contact, support, sympathy, all without ever thinking about it. That it was needed and appreciated didn't have to be said out loud.

"How does Ross fit in?"

"I'd known Ross casually for years. Our families were friends. After it all happened, he was there for me. Familiar, dependable—or so I thought. I went to work raising funds for the Cancer Society, and Ross was always around. He was . . ." The adjective eluded her as it had every time she'd tried to sort through her feelings.

"Safe." Wade supplied the word, easily seeing what Bronwynn had turned around and around and was trying to come up with in frustrated confusion.

She went completely still as the word sank in. It was the missing piece to a puzzle. She didn't understand it, but she knew she had the key. Wade had given it to her.

The colors of her eyes were startlingly clear as she

settled her intense gaze on him and said, "Safe. What a terribly interesting word."

"It's only natural to want to hang on to something familiar and unthreatening when it seems as if the world's being torn apart around you."

Bronwynn knew there was much more to it than that, but it certainly was a start. "Yes," she said. "I suppose it is."

Their conversation was interrupted by the arrival of the express delivery truck. Duty bound, Murphy had shipped the thick packet of reports Wade had requested, but true to his own conscience, he had included a note telling his boss and friend to take it easy. His suggestion that Wade read while stretched out in a hammock with a tall, cool drink at his elbow brought a smile to Wade's lips.

Bronwynn, on the other hand, was frowning. The sheaf of papers Wade held looked like the unabridged manuscript of *War and Peace*. She didn't think much of the invisible Murphy, who had sent his vacationing boss a mountain of work.

"I'll get to this later," Wade said, tossing the report on a lawn chair. "We should finish up the yard. I'm sure you've got other work to do today."

"Work, work, work," Bronwynn said, only half-teasing, hands on her hips. "That's all you ever think about, Wade. You're such a stuffed shirt."

He looked astounded by her evaluation. "I am not a stuffed shirt!"

"Ha! You've been on vacation for days and you only just managed to stop wearing a necktie! If your shirt gets stuffed any fuller, they'll hear the seams splitting in Cleveland." Her gaze scanned the lawn for some way to prove her point and distract him from the report he'd temporarily set aside. "When was the last time you climbed a tree?"

"What?" By the look he gave her she might have

asked him when was the last time he'd grown a second head.

"When was the last time you climbed a tree?" She repeated the question the same way she would for a half-wit.

Wade shrugged and scowled in irritation. "I don't know. I'm a responsible man with a very important job. I don't have time to run around climbing trees."

Bronwynn cupped a hand to her ear. "Is that a seam I hear giving way or is it stuffing rustling?"

Wade's expression suggested it was feathers ruffling— his. Of course he didn't go around climbing trees. What sane person did? Even as he thought about how ridiculous it was, he set off across the lawn behind Bronwynn.

Her purposeful stride took her around the back of the house to what she instantly recognized as a perfect tree for climbing. It had been years since she'd made use of one, but she wasn't about to tell Wade. She grabbed hold of a low limb and swung herself up. Some skills, such as bike riding and tree climbing, never were forgotten, Bronwynn thought. As a child she had alternated regularly between being all sugar and spice and the tomboy terror of the neighborhood. The old skills came back to her with a pleasant rush of nostalgia as she scrambled into the higher branches of the tree.

Wade stared up at her with mingled disbelief, admiration, and exasperation. She had settled herself on a limb and looked down at him through the canopy of leaves, a smudge of dirt and a look of satisfaction on her face. Figuring his pride was on the line if nothing else, Wade got a firm grasp on the same low branch she'd used and hauled himself into the tree, breathing in the rich green scent and remembering long, carefree summers in Indiana.

How long had it been since he'd felt carefree? he wondered. It was in another lifetime it seemed. How long had it been since he'd indulged a boyish sense of adventure and done something that was productive only in bringing a sheen of sweat to his skin and a sense of exhilaration to his soul? Since he'd become a man, too long ago. Bronwynn had teased him into it, and he was grateful to her.

"Stuffed shirt?" he questioned, standing on a branch a few feet below her perch. They were nose to nose as he planted a steadying hand on either side of her bottom.

Bronwynn laughed, delighted. "Maybe there's hope for you after all, Grayson."

He leaned toward her, his gaze narrowing, focusing on her wide, soft mouth. The air around them began to heat. "Is there a kiss for me too? I think I deserve a reward for risking life and limb."

He didn't give her time to answer. It would have been a waste of time anyway, Bronwynn thought to herself as Wade's lips gently captured hers. Anticipation had been simmering inside her ever since the quick kiss he'd surprised her with earlier that morning. It had never stopped simmering since the first kiss they'd shared, the kiss that had stripped pretenses and exposed needs and desires.

She dropped one hand from the limb she was holding, sliding her fingers through Wade's hair to cup the back of his head and draw him closer. She deepened the kiss, her tongue meeting his eagerly. They tasted and tempted, and just when she was on the verge of vertigo, Wade altered the rules, upped the ante.

His mouth trailed heat down her slender throat, over the worn, faded fabric of her purple T-shirt to the hard peak of her breast. Bronwynn grasped the limb above her head, arching toward Wade as she gasped for air. He drew her nipple into his mouth, sucking at her through the cotton, his tongue teasing the hard bud. A soft moan floated up out of her from the warm, tight ache swirling deep in her belly. Her eyes drifted shut as the mists of passion blurred her vision.

Wade wanted all of her. Now. A sudden, overpowering hunger for Bronwynn hit him broadside and knocked his capacity for logical thinking out of commission. Completely forgetting where they were, he tried to take a half step closer to her. The only toehold his sneaker found was air. In the automatic attempt to catch himself, his other foot slipped on the rough bark, and he half-fell, half-sat down on the branch. A soft red haze filled his head as his breath left him on a painful "ooof." The old tree groaned a protest, but the thick branch held.

"Wade? Are you all right?" Bronwynn held on to the tree trunk and leaned down, trying to get a closer look at his face. His eyes were squeezed shut and he was baring his teeth.

"Aarrgh . . ." He let his head fall sideways against the tree. "I may never play the whoopy cushion again."

"I can't imagine you ever played it before."

"Well, now I may never get the chance."

Bronwynn heaved an impatient sigh. "In other words, all you got is a pain in your posterior."

"And I thought that was your job," Wade said dryly.

"Don't take it out on me. You brought this on yourself. You're the one who had to go and get smoochy in a tree."

"Smoochy?" He arched a brow at her. "And who led the way up this tree? Never mind. You'll find a way to make that my fault too."

"It was," she said as she watched him descend. His hand slipped on the next to the last branch, and, with a strangled cry, he dropped to the ground, landing on his feet, but instantly keeling over with a dramatic groan.

Bronwynn scrambled down after him, her heart in her throat. He looked hurt this time. Actually, he looked dead. Never taking her eyes off him, she missed getting her hand on the last branch and dropped out of the tree, landing on Wade.

"Oooofff!"

"Oh, Wade, thank God you're not dead!"

"I'll thank God when you get your elbow out of my solar plexus," he said, his voice a gravelly growl. This wasn't quite what he'd had in mind when he'd staged his dramatic dismount from the tree.

Bronwynn rearranged herself on top of him, brushing his hair out of his eyes. "You scared me."

"Did I?" he asked softly, looking up into her earnest green and blue eyes. "I'm sorry."

Framing her face with his hands, he brought her mouth down to his and kissed her deeply, gently, marveling at her texture and taste. She was so responsive, so giving. A shaft of anger stabbed him at the thought that some man had her sweetness and openness offered to him and had carelessly abused them.

"Is this a good place to get smoochy?" he asked with a chuckle.

Bronwynn's lips hovered just above his, ready to lower the fraction of an inch necessary to make contact. She snuggled her body on top of him, feeling his lean, hard strength. His arousal was pressed between them, reminding her of everything masculine about him and everything feminine about herself. The thoughts warmed her from the inside out until she felt as pliant and soft as bread dough. "This is a wonderful place to get smoochy."

Taking her mouth again, Wade rolled her beneath him on the cool, shaded grass. She cradled him between her legs, hips arching instinctively against his hardness. Instantly the kiss turned wild, almost rough, almost out of control. Wade raised his head, stunned by and trembling because of the force of the feelings she unleashed in him. He'd never felt so close to the edge, so close to losing his coolheaded command of the situation.

He looked down at her with something akin to wonder in his eyes. "Oh, Bronwynn, I want to take you to bed."

Her breath caught in her throat. The pounding of her heart knocked it loose again. She stared up at Wade, trying to decipher the look of near-frustration on his face. "Is that a problem?"

"Yes," he said, nipping at her chin. "I don't think I can make it that far. I want you too much."

Her smile was naturally seductive. Her hands kneaded at the tension in his shoulders. "Then let's not wait."

"You want to make love here?" he asked, his hands sneaking down to the hem of her T-shirt. "In the grass?"

"Why not?" She dragged his polo shirt up his back, her fingers taking time out to explore the smooth skin that had been uncovered just above the waistband of his jeans.

"Someone might see us." He bit his lip at the wonderful sensation of her hands on his back.

Bronwynn's respiration had become uneven. She didn't notice. Her attention was focused solely on the man above her. "This is Vermont, Wade, there isn't anybody around to see us."

"You know," he said with a devastatingly sexy smile, "I'm growing rather fond of Vermont."

They managed to laugh and kiss and work each other's shirts up at the same time. Impatiently Wade yanked his over his head and tossed it aside. He kneeled over Bronwynn and his hands stilled just below her breasts. The humor left his face.

"Is this too soon for you?" He had to ask while he still had a scrap of sanity left. If she said it was too soon, that she really wasn't ready, he would get up and walk away. He wouldn't be happy about it, but he would do it. He wouldn't take advantage of her vulnerability.

Bronwynn looked up at him. Too soon? No. She had learned time should be measured by its quality not quantity. They had shared with each other, cared for each other. She felt closer to him than she ever had felt to Ross. But it was just like Wade to ask, to give her the chance to change her mind before she had any regrets. He might have had the exterior of a world-weary cynic, but he had the soul of Lancelot—honorable, compassionate, good. Reaching up to touch his cheek, she felt something in her heart give way and turn warm.

"No, it's not too soon." In fact the timing was just right, she thought as Wade discarded her T-shirt.

"I thought you were swearing off men for at least a year," he said, his hands returning to cup her breasts.

Bronwynn thought she would faint. "I guess I was mistaken," she murmured.

Kneeling, they tried to kiss and help each other out of jeans and underwear at the same time. They ended up on the grass, giggling, tangled hopelessly in each other's pants. Once the clothing had been dispensed with, however, play turned quickly to passion.

Bronwynn gave without reserve, without inhibition. Her hands and mouth were eager in their pursuit of places Wade liked to be touched and teased. He was ticklish in the tender crease where thigh met hip. Closing her hand around his arousal caused him to tense every muscle in his body until he quivered like a bow-string. She dragged her tongue over his flat brown nipple and trembled in anticipation as she heard him groan.

His control slipping away from him like a rope through wet hands, Wade rolled Bronwynn to her back and pinned her there with his own weight. Her silky legs ran up and down along his hair-roughened ones. Her hips lifted against his, cushioning his manhood in her nest of flame curls. The tips of her small round breasts burrowed through his chest hair to tease him. Even though they were in the shade of the tree they'd climbed, he felt heat searing his skin, as if the fever of passion would consume him body and soul.

His hand skimmed down her side, over her slender hip to a length of creamy thigh that took his breath away, returning to cup her breast and lift it to his mouth. As he teased her nipple with his teeth, he slid his hand down across her flat belly. His fingers combed through the thicket of curls to the warm, moist secrets that lay beyond. As she murmured his name, her hand closed over his, guiding him, showing him what she liked, arousing him further, until the final frayed threads of control eluded his grasp.

With a deep sound of masculine need rumbling low in his chest, Wade kneed Bronwynn's thighs apart, lifted her hips to his, and plunged into her, deep and hard. Afraid he might have hurt her, he froze as her nails dug into his back, but the look on her face was exultant. Slowly he withdrew and repeated the process again and again.

Bronwynn let the feelings swamp her—joy, rightness, pleasure beyond anything she'd ever known. The sensations washed over her then spiraled down into a whirlpool that tightened and intensified deep in the most feminine part of her, in the hot, satiny sheath Wade had filled with the most masculine part of him. She pulled him down and wrapped her arms around him as he moved in and out of her, and held on when the waves of ecstasy hit them both.

Long minutes later, Wade raised his head slowly to gaze down at Bronwynn. His thick, tawny hair finally had decided to carry out its threat to be unruly. It tumbled across his forehead, lending a roguish quality to his clean-cut good looks. The combination made Bronwynn's heart thud.

"You were right," he whispered, combing a twig out of her brilliant red hair with his fingers. "This is a good place to get smoochy."

As if to prove his point, a breeze snuck under the tree and cooled the sweat on his back. Not quite capable of speech yet, Bronwynn only smiled lazily. She felt boneless and wonderful. Wade rolled off her, and they stretched out side by side, naked in the grass, recovering from the passion that had overwhelmed them both. They were silent, each unknowingly contemplating the same question. Why?

Why this woman? he asked himself. This woman with the mismatched cat eyes, who could so easily annoy and exasperate him. Why had she been the one to take him someplace no other woman ever had? He'd had his share of women, had thought himself a good lover. He'd pleased and been pleased, but he had never experienced what he'd just shared with Bronwynn. It hadn't been merely a satisfying physical release. It had been much more. Why?

Why this man? she asked herself. This man who was so unlike her. Why had he been able to make her feel something the man she'd nearly married never had? She was a woman who knew herself very well and was comfortable with herself. But she didn't have the answer to her question, and she wondered why she felt as if it were a secret.

Wade levered himself up to a sitting position and reached for his shorts. He smiled softly. "It would be too easy to stay here all day." He stood up and tugged the snug white briefs into place. "We've got work to finish, and I've got to tackle that report."

Bronwynn scowled at him, before and after she had tugged her T-shirt over her head. "Crack that whip. An hour's relaxation on vacation. How could we have been so frivolous?"

Pulling her into his arms, he smacked her bare bottom playfully. "I wouldn't call what we've been doing relaxing. Frankly, you wore me out."

"Is that a fact?" Bronwynn nibbled at his lower lip

between giggles. Darn the man, he'd discovered every ticklish spot she had. "If you'd quit smoking, you'd have enough energy left to spend another hour under this tree."

"I've never heard a better incentive to quit in my life." He caught her hands as she started to drag his shorts back down. "Behave yourself. We can't spend the entire afternoon on smoochy pursuits."

"I don't see why not." She pouted a little as she pulled her jeans on, her look gaining Wade's full attention as he zipped up his fly.

He wagged a finger at her. "Don't give me that look. I know that look, Bronwynn."

"What look?" she asked, letting her full lower lip droop just a bit more.

"That look." Wade set his chin at a stubborn angle and looked as if he were ready to start pacing. "I'm not giving in. I mean it."

She gave a little sigh and tried batting her eyelashes at him, hoping she didn't look as if she'd just lost a contact lens. She'd never been much on coy seduction. She took a step toward him. He took a step back.

"You think I'm a pushover," Wade said, his fingers lingering on his zipper. "I'm not."

"No," she said in her most disappointed tone. "I guess you're not."

"No, I'm no pushover." He scowled at her for a minute longer. Her expression made him feel as if he'd cast her out of her home into a cold wet rain. Wade yanked his zipper down with one hand and pulled Bronwynn to him with the other. "Just remember that."

"I will," she said, smiling against his lips.

When they finally made it out from under the tree, the afternoon was half-gone. Wade grumbled good-naturedly as they walked hand in hand around the side of the house to the patio. Spending the day making love with Bronwynn on the cool grass in the shade of a tree hadn't exactly been torture. He did, however, intend to get to the report Murphy had sent up.

The report Bronwynn's sheep was eating the final pages of.

Muffin munched contentedly on the proposed defense budget, the chewed-off end of her tether dragging on the ground. She turned and bleated a greeting to Wade and her mistress. Tucker sat on one of the chairs at the table, trying to appear innocent.

Wade glared at the sheep. "How would you like to change her name to Leg of Lamb?"

Bronwynn pressed her fingertips to her lips and tried rather unsuccessfully not to laugh. She picked up the sheep's rope and looked the animal in the eye. "Muffin, you naughty girl."

"Scolding is usually more effective if you don't giggle between each word," Wade said dryly.

"I'm sorry." She giggled, then bit it back. "We're sorry. Really."

Hands on his hips, Wade glanced away. He should have been furious. He'd gone to a lot of trouble to have the report delivered, now a sheep had eaten it. He tried to hold back the bubble of laughter, but it wasn't possible. He glanced at Bronwynn and let it go, shaking his head.

"I guess the Defense Department will still be there when I get back."

Seven

Wade cast a dubious look at the contraption Bronwynn cradled in her arms. "Are you sure this is necessary? Couldn't you just call a game warden?"

Bronwynn stared purposefully at the weathered old carriage house that was situated some thirty or forty yards behind the main house. Neglect of the grounds had allowed the woods to creep in behind the carriage house, but she intended to remedy the situation as soon as she got around to figuring out how to run a chain saw.

"It's necessary and it's personal. Those little bandits ripped a hole in my new screen door and made off with a whole box of glazed doughnuts and a bag of Double Stuff Oreos."

"Oooh." Wade narrowed his eyes and planted his hands on his hips. "Them's fightin' words."

Bronwynn made a face and giggled at him. It always tickled her to hear Wade laugh, to see the lines of strain and worry vanish from his face. More than a week had passed since they'd become lovers, and she was more determined than ever to see to it he got the break from work he needed so badly.

She had become a regular magician when it came to making his cigarettes disappear. She was subtle about it, sneaking four or five away here and there, then keeping Wade too distracted to notice. Bronwynn figured he'd cut down by a third at least. She was hoping he would cut down even more on his own once she gave him her little gift—a case of Pierson's sugarless gum.

Antacid tablets were becoming a rare sight as well. The bonus was that she was learning how to cook while making sure Wade got at least two decent meals a day. And, since she had offered to do his grocery shopping along with her own, his kitchen was stocked with healthy foods, while items such as coffee and frozen Mexican dinners were "accidentally" forgotten.

If he realized he was being cleverly manipulated toward good health, Wade didn't let on. Of course, he'd been too busy insisting on helping with her projects around the house. Bronwynn was perfectly capable of tackling most of the jobs herself, with the help of a how-to book she'd picked up at Hank's Hardware, but Wade, in his typical grumbling fashion, always managed to "give in" and help her. By letting him help her, she actually was helping Wade. He couldn't very well stick his nose in a report on U.S. involvement in Central America if he was up to his elbows in paint stripper.

Now he had begrudgingly volunteered to help her capture her resident marauders—a pair of young raccoons that had holed up in the carriage house.

"We have to get them out of here," she said. "It's not just a matter of food. It's a matter of my Mercedes. I want to clean this shed out and use it as a garage. I like animals, but not enough to give them my car. Besides, they'll probably be happier in the woods, don't you think?"

"Sure," Wade said straight-facedly. "I know I'd be

happier having to forage for grubs and raw fish than I would be eating free junk food."

Bronwynn frowned and hefted the cage into a more comfortable position in her arms. "Anyway, Wizzer will know what to do with them."

"Make a coat? A pair of caps?" Wade grinned at her expression. He enjoyed teasing her. It had been eons since he'd known a woman he would have even thought of teasing. Bronwynn was a dose of fun he hadn't realized he'd needed. He had thought everything was the way he wanted it—until he'd found Bronwynn. "Who is this Wizzer guy anyway?"

"I told you, he's a hermit I met while I was taking a walk in the woods the other day."

"Oh, yeah." He wrinkled his nose. "The one who gave you that god-awful insect repellent."

"The repellent happens to be made of all natural ingredients," she informed him.

Wade snorted. "So is horse manure."

With a disgusted look, she heaved the cage into Wade's arms and started for the door of the carriage house. She shot him a considering glance over her shoulder. "It'll do you some good to meet Wizzer."

It took the better part of three hours to cage the raccoons. They set the trap, baited with bread and blueberry jam, on top of Uncle Duncan's old DeSoto, next to a row of shelves Bronwynn had seen the creatures scurrying along. Then they hid in the musty shadows and waited, passing the time necking. At long last, the raccoons gave in to temptation and the cage door closed behind them.

Bronwynn and Wade each grabbed one of the handles on the side of the trap and, with their furry prisoners hissing and growling between them, headed into the woods on an old overgrown trail.

"I had a coonskin cap when I was a kid," Wade reminisced. He took in the lush green scenery as they walked, breathing in the rich, damp scents. From the corner of his eye he saw a deer duck back into thicker foliage. "It got mange or something. My mom made me throw it out."

Bronwynn looked down at the raccoons. While one was trying to unfasten the cage door with his spindly little fingers, the other stared up at her with curious, bright black eyes shining behind his mask. His button nose twitched at her as he poked it between the wires of the trap. He sat back on his haunches and let out a shrill whinny. He was adorable. How could anyone think of making a cap out of him, she wondered.

"Bronwynn," Wade said in a warning tone. "You're getting that look. Stop it. You can't keep coons as pets; they're wild."

"I know. I was just thinking how glad I am Fess Parker is selling real estate now instead of encouraging people to wear wildlife on their heads." One coon— Bronwynn had already started thinking of them as Bob and Ray—offered the other a piece of the bread and jam that had been their undoing. Her heart twisted. "Aren't they sweet?"

"They stink, honey. Use the olfactory system God gave you."

The look on her face as she stared down at the little animals was almost enough to make him turn around and head back to Foxfire. Next she'd have him building her a little raccoon chalet. Why did he have to be such a soft touch? The Pillsbury Doughboy was tougher than he was. He tried to concentrate on an image of raccoons tearing up the upholstery of her gorgeous red Mercedes. "They belong in the wild, sweetheart."

"Yeah, that's what Wizzer said." She brightened as she caught sight of a grizzled head some distance down the path as strains of an old Beach Boys tune reached her ears. "There he is now."

Wade stopped in his tracks and stared at the wild-looking old coot, then turned to Bronwynn, incredulous. "You thought I was a serial killer when we met, but you made friends with him? Jeez, Bronwynn. He looks like something out of one of those teenage horror movies."

Suddenly he was angry with her for having gone walking in the woods alone. Anything could have happened to her. Forgetting about the way she had crowned him with the soda cans the first night, he decided her innate naïveté prevented her from thinking about things such as killer bears and weird old geezers who did people in and made lamp shades out of them. His stomach knotted at the thought of anything happening to Bronwynn. Hadn't he known all along she needed a keeper?

"Don't go spastic on me, Wade. Wizzer's okay." She waved a greeting. "Hi, Wizzer!"

"Red!" the old man called in a booming voice, two thousand dollars worth of capped teeth flashing white in the nest of his salt-and-pepper beard.

"He calls me Red," Bronwynn said in an aside to Wade. She shot him a warning look. "Don't get any ideas about that, Grayson."

Wade was too caught up in staring at Wizzer. Since when did hermits cap their teeth? he asked himself. The older man might have been sixty, he might have been seventy, but he didn't top six feet, and he was built like a fireplug. A wild cloud of hair swirled around his head and onto his shoulders. It would have been difficult to say where the hair ended and the beard began. A Princeton T-shirt spanned his thick chest and stretched over shoulders that were layered with the kind of muscle that came from swinging an axe. He wore a red plaid kilt and argyle wool knee socks. When they set down the coon cage, he engulfed Bronwynn in an exuberant bear hug.

"Wizzer, this is my friend, Wade Grayson," Bronwynn

said when he let her go and she could breathe again. "Wade, meet Wizzer Bralower."

Wade's jaw dropped. "Wizzer—*Alastair* Bralower? The Wizard of Wall Street?"

"Guilty!" Wizzer grinned and laughed as if it were a huge joke. He clasped Wade's hand in a lumberjack grip. "Good to meet you, Wade. Red tells me you're a congressman. I don't keep up on political stuff anymore. Hell, you look like a Beach Boy. You don't happen to know all the words to 'Little Deuce Coupe,' do you?"

"Ah—no."

Wade was astounded. People had been looking for this man for years, and there he was in the backwoods of Vermont wearing a kilt. Obviously he'd flipped out. Wade shook his head. "You just vanished. There were rumors you'd been kidnapped by the Soviets to mastermind a financial takeover of the Western world."

Wizzer made a rude sound. "What a pile of toadstools. Typical, though, I suppose." Offering no explanation for his disappearance, he hunkered down by the cage. "So these are the little bandits?"

"Bob and Ray," Bronwynn said, giving in to her need to name the critters.

While Wizzer and Bronwynn discussed the raccoons, Wade looked around. They had reached a clearing in the woods no bigger than the parking lot of a fast-food restaurant. To one side of the path stood an honest-to-goodness log cabin. An old whiskey keg sat at one corner, ready to collect rainwater from the roof. There was a pile of split wood and a wide stump with an axe stuck in it. Some distance from the cabin a black iron kettle hung over a smoldering fire. A neatly hoed garden was fenced off with chicken wire. It was hardly the setting in which one expected to find a stock market tycoon.

"I know just the place for these little fur balls, Red,"

Wizzer said, offering the raccoons a piece of beef jerky from the leather pouch that hung at his waist. "There's a stream not far from here with plenty of fish and plenty of cover on the bank. Raccoon paradise. They'll love it."

Wade and Bronwynn trudged along behind with the captive coons as Wizzer led the way through the woods, singing "Surfin' USA." When the cage was opened at last, and Bob and Ray scampered off, Bronwynn had to fight back tears. Wade sighed in resignation and reached for her hand. What a funny little witch his Bronwynn was, he thought.

His Bronwynn. He liked the sound of that, but what would Bronwynn think? She had let go of her idea of swearing off all men. They had established a relationship neither of them had tried to name yet, a relationship neither had been looking for. Would she shy away if she knew he was feeling possessive? It scared *him* a bit. He had never allowed a woman to get close to him. His work had come first, above everything, including his own health, he was realizing slowly.

Every day since he'd become involved with Bronwynn he'd been at war with himself. Part of him demanded he give his attention to the work he'd brought along with him. Part of him said the work could wait until after he'd seen Bronwynn and rescued her from whatever mischief she'd managed to get herself into. Two weeks earlier he had fallen asleep worrying about the federal deficit, now Bronwynn was his first thought in the morning and his last at night.

He was a good congressman, conscientious, dedicated. Was there room in his life for a distraction like Bronwynn Prescott Pierson? He tried to imagine going back to his drab apartment in Alexandria and the life he'd had before Vermont, and felt strangely empty.

He'd been bewitched by a pair of parti-colored eyes, he thought, frowning to himself as he trailed behind.

Bronwynn was walking arm in arm with Wizzer, asking him a million questions about the different plants along the trail. Like a curious child, she had to touch and smell them all. Twice Bralower had to save her from sticking her patrician nose into some nasty poison ivy or itch weed. Wade just shook his head and tried to steer his mind toward thoughts of the next superpower summit, but the closest his brain came to thinking about Russia was picturing Bronwynn stretched out naked on a sable throw.

When they got back to Wizzer's cabin, Bralower invited them in for tea. The cabin was one spacious room, neat as a pin with blue Priscilla curtains at the windows and drying herbs hanging from the rafters. A stone fireplace dominated one end of the building. One wall was lined with bookshelves that were crammed with books on herbology, natural remedies, theology, and mythology. Sitting on the quilt-covered bed was an enormous blue tabby cat that looked as if it weighed about twenty pounds. Tufts of hair stuck out of his ears. His tail was a plume of long fluffy fur.

"That's Thoreau," Wizzer said by way of introduction. "Big sucker, isn't he? He's a Maine coon cat."

Bronwynn went pale, her freckles standing out in sharp relief across her nose as she stared into the cat's wide gold eyes. "A coon? . . . He wouldn't—I mean, you wouldn't let him—"

"Hang loose, Red," Wizzer said with a chuckle as he poured their tea into stoneware mugs with pictures of Garfield on them. "It's just a name. He wouldn't know a coon from a crocodile, but he's death on mice."

They all sat down at the scarred pine table. Bralower studied Wade. Wade stared back with frank speculation in his eyes, wondering whether or not he would get a straight answer if he asked the man what he was doing there.

Finally Wizzer let loose a full-bodied laugh. "All right,

College Boy, it's plain you're dying to know, so I'll tell you. I lost everything in the last big stock market crash." He glanced around his tidy cabin with a smile. "Can't say that I miss any of it. I wasn't really happy. I'd gotten too caught up in it—the work, the pressure. I didn't even realize it until I'd gotten out."

Bronwynn nodded sagely, her gaze on Wade. "Couldn't see the forest for the woods."

"Trees," Wade corrected automatically.

Wizzer laughed and slapped him on the back hard enough to collapse a lung. "Don't sweat the petty things, College Boy."

"But what do you do out here?" Wade asked hoarsely, wondering if there was a big handprint permanently branded into his back.

"I live. I garden. I contemplate mankind and the power of myth." He opened a drawer that ran the length of the table, pulled out a shiny brass cylinder, and handed it to Wade. "In my spare time I build kaleidoscopes."

Wade raised the toy to his eye and looked through at the brilliant colored patterns. Each one seemed to be trying to outdo the last as he rotated the cylinder. His logical mind knew he was looking at nothing more than the reflections of bits of colored glass, that a kaleidoscope was nothing more than a pair of mirrors and a couple of lenses. In his heart as he looked at the bright, pretty colors he thought of Bronwynn and magic.

His heart lodged in his throat. It wasn't at all like him to be whimsical. What was she doing to him, he wondered as he lowered the kaleidoscope and looked at Bronwynn. She was busy gazing into another of Wizzer's creations, one with a polished wood cylinder. Her face was alight as if she'd never seen anything so wondrous or beautiful. She was wealthy enough to buy herself virtually anything she wanted, yet she was enchanted by something as simple as the toy she held.

After they'd finished their herbal tea and snacked on bread made from some part of a thistle, Wade and Bronwynn headed back down the trail toward Foxfire, leaving Wizzer behind them brewing dandelion wine and singing "Surfin' Safari."

"Well," Wade said as they stepped out of the woods into Bronwynn's backyard. "I should go home and get a little studying done."

Bronwynn stepped in front of him to open the gate of Muffin's pen—one of Wade's first projects—glad he couldn't see her expression. If she ever got her hands on that Murphy character, he was going to be one sorry son of a gun. Three days after Muffin had eaten Wade's Pentagon report another one had shown up. She'd been doing her darndest to distract Wade from it ever since.

Forcing a light tone, she said, "Okay. Thanks for helping with Bob and Ray."

Wade frowned as he watched her unhook the sheep's gate. Muffin bleated an excited greeting, rubbed her head against the leg of Bronwynn's jeans on the way out of her pen, then stopped and fixed Wade with an imperious glare before moving on to join Tucker under a maple tree.

"I'd hang around and help you with the house, but I really need to get through that report."

Bronwynn shot him an absent smile then bent to check on the sheep's water bucket. "That's fine, Wade. I understand."

"We can't all drop out on our responsibilities the way Alastair Bralower did," he said testily.

"Nope, we can't." She hooked the gate open so Muffin could go in and out as she chose. "Of course, some of us try for a balance. And then some of us . . . don't."

Wade planted his hands on his hips. He scowled as she exited the pen. "My work is important, Bronwynn."

"I never said it wasn't." She dismissed the topic with a bland smile she knew was setting Wade's teeth on edge. She almost could hear him grinding the enamel off. "I won't be able to have dinner with you unless we make it late. I rented a steamer from Hank. I'm going to remove the old wallpaper in the kitchen. Once I get going I know I won't want to stop until I'm finished." She pressed a quick kiss to his cheek. "See you later."

Wade watched her start toward the back porch, her long, slim legs carrying her gracefully away from him. What could Bronwynn possibly know about running a steamer? Probably about as much as she knew about patching holey jeans. The ones she was wearing were worn out in both knees, and one spot on her delectably rounded derriere was held together by single strands of fraying white thread. When she stooped to examine the rip in her screen door, Wade could see panty lace through the near-tear.

His dark eyebrows drew together in an annoyed stare as he strode across the lawn. "What do you know about running a steamer? Do you have the proper electrical outlets for something like that?"

She shrugged and raked her baby-fine hair back out of her eyes. "I guess. It has three prongs on the plug. All I have to do is find an outlet with three holes, right?"

Wade pressed his eyes closed and shook his head. "I don't know how you ever managed to survive to maturity."

"I guess it was a miracle," Bronwynn said dryly.

An hour later they were in the middle of the hot, dirty job of removing the hideous kitchen wallpaper—or rather, Wade was in the middle of it. Bronwynn, who had changed into a lightweight cotton sundress, was standing in the middle of the kitchen floor with her arms impatiently crossed over her chest, watching Wade take over.

It happened every time. Every time he begrudgingly told her he'd help with a project, he invariably herded her away from the work and ended up doing most of it himself. Bronwynn nipped at her lower lip and told herself it was just as well if it kept Wade away from the pressure cooker of his own work. It was exactly what she wanted to happen, exactly what she had planned to happen. Still, it rankled.

She was caught in a trap of her own making. She played the careless incompetent to insure Wade would take over, but she hated having him think she wasn't capable of handling manual labor. Every once in a while she wanted him to see she could handle the job of renovating Foxfire. What she wanted was to have it both ways. It was Wade's fault she couldn't.

"Chauvinist," she muttered.

"What's that?" Wade called over his shoulder above the hiss of the steamer and the rock music coming from Bronwynn's ever-present boom box.

What the heck, Bronwynn thought mischievously. She took a step closer to the ladder he was standing on and smiled up at him. "I said you're a chauvinist."

Wade looked thunderstruck. He turned the steamer off. "I most certainly am not a chauvinist."

"Are too."

"Am not." Pressing his lips together into a firm line, he broke off the childish bantering. He wagged a finger at her. "I'll have you know I was endorsed by a number of women's organizations."

He was so cute when he got peeved. It was all she could do to keep herself from hugging him. She definitely couldn't resist egging him on. "Oh? Which ones? The League of Women for Congressmen with Cute Butts?"

Try as he might, Wade couldn't form an angry retort.

His reputation was being questioned, but he couldn't quite force himself to get angry about it. He consistently voted for equal opportunity for women, but he was the one holding the wallpaper steamer, wasn't he?

It didn't have anything to do with Bronwynn's gender, he told himself. It had more to do with the fact that Bronwynn plus power tools added up to disaster.

"You want to run the steamer?" he asked. "Do you remember what happened when you wanted to run the carpet cleaner in the parlor?"

"How was I to know that rug was wool?" she asked. "It was ugly anyway."

"And what about the day you wanted to run the electric hedge trimmer?"

"Too much shrubbery distracts from the beauty of the house." Her lips twitched and she gave in to the giggles. Wade laughed along with her. She raised her hands in defeat. "All right, I admit I'm not terribly mechanical."

"Muffin is more mechanical than you are."

He had a valid point. She really wasn't very adept with power tools, even when she was trying to be. She tossed a scrap of wallpaper at him. "Please, Wade, please let me run the steamer," she begged, fighting back laughter. "I'm bored to tears standing down here with nothing to do but clean up the mess."

His gaze was speculative. "Hmmm . . . I don't know. Do you really think I have a cute butt?"

"Hand it over, Grayson," she said sternly.

"Gee, I don't think I can, Bronwynn," he said, peering over his shoulder. He patted a hand to the seat of his jeans. "I'm kind of attached to it."

"I'm going to attach my foot to it in a minute. I rented that darn steamer. I'm not taking it back until I get to use it."

"Okay." He capitulated with a long-suffering sigh.

"But you *will* let me show you how to use it first, and you *will* pay attention."

"I promise."

Instantly she was on the ladder with him, snuggling up against him as she tried to get a good close look at the machine.

"Bronwynn," Wade said, "two people should never be on the same ladder at once."

She made a face. "Wade, you're such a fussbudget. It has to be strong enough to hold us both; our combined weight isn't that much. You know they must build these things strong enough so enormously fat people can use them too. Otherwise it would be discrimination, right?" She snatched the steamer out of Wade's hands and began examining it. "Now, how do you work this puppy?"

As she turned half her attention to the steamer and half to the Springsteen song on the radio, she nearly shoved Wade off the ladder. He grabbed hold of one side and prayed they wouldn't end up on the floor amid a pile of splinters. When he was reasonably certain she could handle the steamer without endangering herself, he climbed down.

"I wonder how Bob and Ray are adjusting to forest life," Bronwynn said as she worked. She paid no mind to the sway of the ladder as she began moving to one of her favorite songs. The possibility of danger never entered her mind—not when she was on a ladder, not when she crossed a Boston street against the light.

"Oh, I imagine all their new animal friends are holding a housewarming for them tonight," Wade said sardonically as he searched through the rubble of junk-food wrappers on the marble-topped work island, looking for his cigarettes.

Watching Bronwynn dance around on the ladder was enough to make him long for a roll of antacid tablets. Oddly enough, he didn't have any with him. He found a half-crumpled pack of cigarettes and extracted a slightly bent one. He lit it, drawing the smoke in deeply as he leaned back against the work island, wondering if it really was only his third of the day.

"Anything would be preferable to being made into a coat," Bronwynn said. 'I'm not much for fur coats myself. They give me the creeps. It makes my skin crawl to think I'm wearing something that used to be alive."

She aimed the steamer at the green wallpaper that sported little copper kettles and crossed forks and spoons. She already had carefully measured the walls and ordered new paper in a dainty country print with a blue background. "I've often wondered about camel hair too. I mean, is it really the hair of camels or is that just a name? Haven't you wondered about that?"

Wade regarded her with a look of puzzlement. If he lived to be a hundred, he'd never figure out the way her mind worked.

Methodically, he tapped ash into a Styrofoam cup and took another long pull on his cigarette. As he exhaled he said, "Bronwynn, I wonder about things like political unrest in the Third World. I don't have time to wonder whether or not my topcoat is courtesy of some hairy hump with legs wandering around the deserts of Saudi Arabia."

"That's the trouble with you, Wade," Bronwynn said, turning on the ladder to face him, one foot dangling in midair. "How are you ever going to be able to solve big problems if you never question the little things?"

The sheet of paper she'd been working at loosening suddenly gave way and crushed over her head like a wall-covering tidal wave. Wade couldn't help but chuckle. Where Bronwynn had stood on the ladder, unaccountably lovely in a dress that hung like a gunny sack on her, was now a pyramid of inside-out wallpaper.

"Okay, Grayson," came a disgruntled mumble. "You've had your little chuckle, now get this thing off me."

"It'll be easier to get *you* out from under *it*."

He lifted the sheet of paper and stepped under it, taking the steamer from Bronwynn and setting it safely out of the way. Getting Bronwynn out of the tangle wasn't so simple. The paper clung tenaciously to the top of her head. Not quite able to see what she was doing, she missed a step as she tried to descend, and she and the ladder parted company. Bronwynn fell into Wade's arms. The domino theory carried them both to the floor, the paper falling over them like a blanket.

"Honey," Wade remarked dryly, his hands running lazily over Bronwynn's supple back, "if you wanted to be on top, all you had to do was tell me."

Bronwynn grinned, looking down at him. She could still make out Wade's handsome, clean-cut features. Her body was pressed along the length of his, leaving no doubt in her mind as to his virility. She arched her hips and gasped as his body responded accordingly. Bronwynn had never thought of herself as a temptress, but Wade brought out latent talents in her. She ran her tongue along her lower lip and said huskily, "I want to be on top."

Wade's breath lodged like two fists in the very bottom of his lungs. With Bronwynn rubbing against him, he was getting hard fast. He wanted her, and he wanted her right away. As usual, he wanted her with an intensity that would startle him when he thought of it afterward. Now he had a difficult time thinking of anything but the way her body felt melting into his. He was a man who was ordinarily in control of every aspect of his life; with Bronwynn he barely knew the meaning of the word.

"I've never gotten smoochy on the kitchen floor under a sheet of wallpaper before," she said, lowering her upper body so her nipples teased him through the thin fabric of her sundress and his shirt. She wanted to feel them naked against the carpet of rough curls on his chest. She wanted to feel his thumbs tease them, his hot mouth close over them.

"Bronwynn," Wade said, his voice full of dark promises as his hands slid over her bottom to the tops of her thighs. His fingers worked the soft cotton of her dress upward. "You're one of a kind."

A pleased smile tilted her lips as she pressed them to Wade's. "Thank you."

He worked her panties down and kneaded the tender flesh of her buttocks. "It wasn't necessarily a compliment. Ouch! No biting!"

With desire preaching urgency, their clothing was dealt with accordingly. She unbuttoned Wade's shirt and pushed it open. He unbuttoned the front of Bronwynn's sundress and pulled the straps down her arms so the fabric pooled at her waist, and her breasts were bared to his gaze and touch. His fingers ran over her bottom, hurrying to explore the moist warmth between her thighs as she leaned over him, offering one taut nipple to his mouth.

Cries and moans caught in her throat and came out as whimpers and sighs as Wade's teeth and lips tugged at her breast. They were well acquainted with each other's bodies and needs, and the heat between them rose quickly to the flash point of passion.

"Oh, Wade, I want you," Bronwynn whispered, dragging kisses down the strong column of his throat. She inhaled his musky masculine scent, then sighed at the feel of his arousal probing gently between her legs, seeking out the aching emptiness he knew would welcome him. "I want you inside me. Deep."

"Then take me, sweetheart," he said, reaching between them to position himself for her. "Take all of me. Now."

Bronwynn leaned back and eased down on him slowly, savoring their union an inch at a time, pausing when she was filled with him. Wade's hands splayed at her waist, biting into her flesh when her hips rotated on him. He lifted her, then pulled her back down. She moved on him rhythmically, wantonly, holding nothing back, rushing toward the brilliant burst of fulfillment she knew she would find with Wade—only with Wade.

When it came, the star burst of color in her head was more vivid than that of the kaleidoscope she'd looked through earlier, and it went on and on and on.

Wade let his hands wander up Bronwynn's body. Her skin was hot and damp from the fever of physical need. Her breasts swelled in his hands. He'd forgotten they were lying under a sheet of old kitchen wallpaper. He'd forgotten everything but Bronwynn—her beauty, his wild hunger for her, her unreserved giving, the feeling of her body tightening around his as he throbbed first with need, then with fulfillment. He wanted to tell her everything he was feeling, wanted to put a name to it, but it was so unique in his experience, words escaped him.

Bronwynn knew the word. It tasted sweet on the tip of her tongue. But she didn't say it. She was almost certain she'd fallen in love with Wade Grayson, but experience had left her confused, unsure of her ability to see such things clearly. Undeniably there was something special between them, a bond that went deeper than friendship, a closeness that transcended physical intimacy. Mere attraction would never have withstood their differences of personality and philosophy.

It had to be more. Once she had resolved the questions about her past, she would know. She could sense it.

She smiled at him as he drew her down, inviting her to stretch out on top of him. Her lips hovered just above his, a hair's breadth away from a kiss, when something caught her eye.

"Uh—Wade? We have company," she said, biting back

a chuckle as she peered out from under the tent the old wallpaper had made over them.

Wade twisted his head around to look out the screen door. Two pair of shiny black eyes stared back at him. Tan triangular ears twitched back and forth curiously. Striped tails curved like plumes against the floor of the porch. The little raccoons chattered at each other in what sounded like a comical stage whisper. One sat back on his haunches and whinnied while the other worked his nimble fingers at the new patch in the screen door.

"Apparently, they have no respect for privacy," Wade said, pulling the sheet of wallpaper close around Bronwynn's shoulders.

"What's a little privacy compared to the lure of a bag of Cajun-spice potato chips or a box of Twinkies?" Bronwynn asked, staring at Bob and Ray.

Booming strains of "Fun, Fun, Fun" sounded then, heralding the arrival of yet another guest.

"Great," Wade said, groaning.

Bronwynn's fair complexion blushed a shade that almost matched her hair. She and Wade were on the kitchen floor, wound up in old wallpaper like some kind of weird double mummy. It had been embarrassing enough to have the raccoons see them.

She pressed a quick kiss to his cheek. "This is what we get for being spontaneous."

"There you are, you little bandits," Wizzer said, climbing the porch steps. While they were distracted by the goings on in the kitchen, he snatched up Bob and Ray by the scruff of their necks. He ignored them as they hissed and growled at him, but held them out away from his sides as if they were a pair of buckets.

"Hi, Wizzer," Bronwynn said with a sheepish smile.

"Wizzer," Wade said.

Bralower's brows wriggled like a pair of wooly caterpillars above his glittering blue eyes as he took in the scene on the kitchen floor. His mustache began to twitch. Finally, he gave a great shout of laughter.

"My ex-wife always told me wallpapering was a two-person job." He turned away and headed down the porch steps, kilt swinging jauntily, a squirming raccoon in each hand, his broad shoulders shaking with suppressed laughter. "If only I had known . . ."

Eight

"Blackmail is an ugly thing," Wade said. "Are you sure you want to give in to this, honey?"

Bronwynn looked over her shoulder at him from her perch three steps up on the ladder. "I don't think I have a choice. It's a lot easier for me to give in to their demands than fight them. They won't leave me alone." She stuck three nails between her lips and talked around them. "I'd rather give them a regular supply of cat food than have them raiding my kitchen every night. Wizzer's getting sick of carting them back to the woods. They obviously aren't going to stay out there. Building this little chalet for them will at least keep them out of the carriage house and out of my car. I hope."

Wade leaned back against Bronwynn's pickup, his elbows resting behind him on the hood. He studied the design of her coon chalet with the critical eye of someone who had been forced to take woodshop in high school and had ended up liking it. Her basic plan was a good one. A platform jutted from the side of the carriage house. There would be a ladder leading up to it and a small A-frame shelter on top. Bronwynn was working on the shelter as they chatted.

He was not going to get involved, he told himself resolutely. Bronwynn's little projects, not to mention Bronwynn herself, had distracted him from his own duties too often. In another two weeks he had to be back in Indiana, and he had to be caught up by then. He was going to leave her to her crazy scheme right away and go see to those figures on child care for middle-income families.

His feet didn't move. Wade glanced down at them. The sneakers that had looked so foreign on him the first day he'd worn them were now comfortably broken in, a little battered, a little dirty. His jeans hugged him, the denim bearing the kind of creases that came from frequent wear, lines of light and dark color behind the knees and where thigh met groin.

He wasn't moving, he realized, wasn't rushing back to his house to dig into a pile of paperwork. He was relaxed, truly relaxed. The very thing he had dreaded, the very thing he had been sent up there for had happened. His nerves had unwound—not sprung as he had feared. He actually felt good. He couldn't quite remember the last time he'd popped an antacid tablet. He even had a tan.

And he had Bronwynn to thank.

A little frisson of nerves cracked his calm. Was it acceptable for him to feel so relaxed? Was it going to take away from his job performance if he had a vacation, or was it going to enhance it? What was going to happen if he didn't memorize that massive Pentagon report? he wondered.

Nothing. He was good at his job, knowledgeable about the issues. And he had a staff that was eager to help lighten his load of memorizing facts and figures. He never had been expected to shoulder the burden alone by anyone—except himself.

He focused his attention on Bronwynn who was getting ready to nail on one side of her raccoon retreat.

Her flame-red hair was caught up in a haphazard ponytail. She wore indecently short cutoffs that displayed
her long legs to perfection. An old royal blue bowling-
team shirt completed the outfit.

What was he going to do about her? The thought of
leaving her behind didn't exactly overjoy him. His mouth
tilted at one corner in a wry smile. He'd certainly made
an about-face for someone who had sworn up and
down he didn't want to get involved with a squirrelly
redhead, even if she did have the greatest legs this side
of Hollywood. He was involved now. He was in deep.

But how deep was Bronwynn in? Was it fair of him
to expect any kind of commitment from her so soon
after her catastrophe with Ross Hilliard? And what
about Foxfire? She loved the place, needed it for a
sense of stability and a sense of purpose. Would she
leave it if he asked her? If they pursued their relationship, would it survive outside Vermont, or would their
differences ultimately pull them apart?

He didn't have the answers to those questions. What
he did know was she was sweet and caring. She was
close to being certifiable, which made her exasperating
but infinitely interesting to be with. She was fresh and
innocent and just looking at her made him hard and
hungry.

Wade tore his gaze from the backs of her knees and
focused on her hands in an attempt to head off the
rush of desire that was shooting from the pit of his
belly to his brain.

"You've got too much angle," he said. "You'll have an
A with a left-handed slant if you leave it that way."

Automatically Bronwynn moved the piece of particle-
board and glanced over her shoulder at Wade for his
approval. She narrowed her eyes as she watched him
light a cigarette, turning back to her project as he
raised his head. Wade watched her carelessly plant a
nail. Singing along with the radio, she swung the ham-

mer with gusto, narrowly missing her thumb and the nail.

"Let me do it," he grumbled, grinding his cigarette out on a rust spot on the Blue Bomb. "We'd both be better off if I never let you get your hand on a tool."

Bronwynn hopped down from the ladder and gave him a sexy smile. "That's not what you said last night."

Wade snaked an arm around her waist as she brushed against him on her way past. "Vixen." The word came on a hoarse chuckle from low in his throat as he nipped at the side of her neck.

Bronwynn hugged herself on her way to sit on the hood of the truck. She loved the tingles that raced over her whenever Wade touched her. For that matter, he didn't have to touch her to set them off. It took nothing more than a smoldering look from his whiskey-colored eyes, or a word in his smoke-edged voice. He made her feel things she had never felt with any other man.

The question was, what was she going to do about it? She knew perfectly well Wade's presence in the house down the road was only temporary. He would be going back to Indiana soon, then back to his high-pressure position in the nation's capital. What would become of the relationship they'd begun? She couldn't think of it as a short-term affair. Wade meant much more to her than a great sex partner and irascible yet pleasant company. She wanted to believe she was in love with him, but uncertainty held her back. Even if she had been able to say for certain, it didn't guarantee Wade would feel the same way.

How many times had he pointed out their differences? He was intense, staid, and career oriented. She had always coasted, letting life take care of itself, and, while she hadn't precisely flaunted convention, she certainly didn't follow it rigidly. Could she fit into Wade's ultraconservative world? More importantly, would he feel comfortable with her there?

Of great interest to her was the fact that she had never really worried about how she would have fit in with Ross's colleagues. She hadn't wondered, not because Ross had given her any assurances, but because it hadn't been important to her—just as Ross hadn't been important to her in the way he should have been.

Oh, Lord, she'd tricked herself into thinking she had loved Ross when she hadn't. Now she wanted to believe she was in love with Wade. What if she wasn't? What if she was? How was she supposed to know for sure?

She pulled a granola bar out of her hip pocket, tore open the wrapper, and bit into it. Chewing thoughtfully, she wondered if it was possible that she wanted to be in love, needed to be in love to fill the void her parents had left when they'd died. Wade had pointed out that Ross had been safe, that she had used him as an emotional anchor at a turbulent time in her life. Was Wade serving the same purpose? Was she going to make a habit of using men as toeholds to get her up the rocky slopes life placed in front of her?

No, she thought. What she felt for Wade was too strong, too unexpected. She had come to Vermont wanting nothing to do with any man. Wade had come right out and said he wanted nothing to do with her. They had become involved almost in spite of themselves. That fact alone was a testimony to how real their feelings for each other were. Wasn't it?

"Have you decided what you're going to do with the house yet?" Wade asked, hoping he sounded more nonchalant than he felt. He glanced over his shoulder. Bronwynn's expression was unusually somber.

"Not precisely. There's still so much work to be done, I figure I have plenty of time to make up my mind." She looked at the house. Next week she had a crew coming to install new windows. Soon the sagging porch would be repaired and the rotting gingerbread trim replaced.

Then the exterior would be painted while she continued work inside.

Pete Lewandowski, a local handyman, was, at the moment, on a scaffold on the far end of the house, using a small torch to strip the layers of alligatored paint off the ornate wide-board trim. Bronwynn had watched him for part of the morning, as he patiently heated the thick crust of paint then scraped it off.

"You think you'll stay here awhile, then?" Wade asked.

Unless you ask me to leave with you. "Yes. You know I love it here."

"Yes, I know." *But would you leave if I asked you to?*

He laid the hammer down and turned to look at her. If he hadn't believed it at first, he believed it now: Bronwynn belonged here. Her privileged birth didn't matter, her high life as an international model didn't matter. She belonged here, just outside Shirley, Vermont, in a house that was part fairy tale, part relic.

Uncomfortable with his intense scrutiny, Bronwynn shrugged, summoning up an impish smile. "It would make a wonderful bed and breakfast inn. Or a home for unwed mothers, or an artists' commune. Or maybe I'll stay here and raise sheep and become an eccentric old maid."

"I can't argue with the eccentric part," Wade said, stepping off the ladder and sauntering toward her. She offered no resistance when he reached up, placed his hands on her waist, and slid her down from the hood of the truck. He pinned her between the Blue Bomb and himself, molding her body to his. "But that old maid business would definitely be a waste."

"You think so?" Her voice sounded as smoky as his.

Wade kneed her thighs apart and stepped between. His hands sliding down her back to her slim hips, he pulled them tight against his own, letting her know how quickly and how intensely she could arouse him.

His mouth took hers in a kiss that was hot and demanding. His tongue slid against its feminine mate, boldly staking claim.

"I want you, Bronwynn," he said, his voice dropping to a guttural growl as he dragged his mouth from hers. Their future together may have been uncertain, but they had here and now.

His fingers speared into her hair, loosing the fine strands from their ponytail. His gaze locked on hers, her eyes so exotic with their almond-shaped tilt. They glittered like jewels—an emerald and a sapphire—glazed with sudden passion. Damn, but she made his blood burn. No other woman had inspired such a reckless sexuality in him. She did it with a look. "I want to take you right now, right here."

"Oh, Wade." A whisper was all she could manage. She suddenly felt about as strong as an overcooked noodle. If Wade hadn't had her locked against him, she probably would have slithered down the side of the truck into a boneless heap on the lawn. She couldn't resist him, and she didn't want to. It didn't matter that a loose piece of chrome was jabbing her in the back.

A wicked chuckle rumbled low in Wade's chest. He ran a hand over her hip and teased the top of her bare thigh with the tips of his fingers. "You've been driving me crazy running around in these cutoffs. Do you have any idea what it does to me to look at your legs?"

"What?" she asked on a breathless whimper.

"It makes me ache to be inside you," he murmured in her ear.

"What's with you two?" a booming voice fairly shouted across the lawn. Wade's head snapped up. Wizzer strode toward them from the woods, his kilt, striped socks, and cotton shirt with billowing sleeves a blaze of red against the green of the forest. His blue eyes twinkled merrily. "Every time I come here I catch you two in a clinch."

"Maybe you ought to call ahead," Wade suggested through gritted teeth. He eased away from Bronwynn to lean his elbows on the hood of the truck. Bronwynn tried to scrub the blush from her cheeks with the heels of her hands.

Wizzer laughed heartily, as if Wade's suggestion was the most absurd thing he'd ever heard. "Where do you suggest I call from?"

Wade flashed his even white teeth. "I hear Rangoon is nice this time of year."

"You want me to go there and miss all this fun?" Wizzer grinned unrepentantly and thumped a hand on the side of the pickup. "Grin and bear it, College Boy. You're young. A little frustration is good for you, keeps you hungry."

Wade's muttered opinion of that bit of wisdom brought another chuckle from the hermit. Mimicking Wade's stance on the other side of the truck, he plunked a plastic container down on the hood and shoved it across. "Hey, Red, did you pick up those batteries for me? I haven't been able to listen to my Beach Boys tapes for two weeks. I've forgotten the words to 'Surfer Girl.' "

Wade peeled back the lid on the container and made a face. "Uck! What is this? It looks like something the cat coughed up."

"Marinated fern fronds," Bronwynn answered. "Wizzer says they'll be good for your stomach."

"As long as I don't eat them," Wade added under his breath as he stared with distaste at the green balls swimming in vinegar.

Bronwynn pinched his bottom. "Don't be such a baby. Did you pick up those batteries?"

"They're in my car."

The three of them strolled to the front of the house where Wade's Lincoln was parked. The driver's door stood open. Tucker sat behind the wheel, panting happily until he saw his master. Immediately he slunk out of the car and crawled under it. Muffin stood on the hood, methodically shredding a carton of cigarettes. She looked up and bleated a greeting with a cigarette dangling from her lip.

Staring into the car at the demolished brown paper bag and the animal footprints all over the beige leather interior, Wade felt his blood pressure skyrocket. He muttered an awe-inspiring string of expletives that rose in a crescendo and concluded with "Four-legged fuzz-ball!"

Like an overprotective mother, Bronwynn rushed forward to place herself between Wade and her pet. Turning around and backing toward the Lincoln, she said, "You must have left the door unlatched."

"That's not the only thing that's unlatched around here," Wade said, fixing her with a burning glare. "Who in her right mind gives a sheep free run of her yard? I sweated for two days building a pen for that rampaging rack of lamb so incidents like this could be avoided."

"You always blame Muffin!" With an indignant sniff, Bronwynn turned and took her sheep by the collar, coaxing her down off the hood of the Lincoln. "Poor Muffin. Some people would rather see you locked up and miserable."

"Some people would rather see her in a crock pot."

Wizzer chuckled at Wade's dry remark and Bronwynn's offended gasp. "I have a great recipe for herbed mutton and new potatoes," he offered.

"Does it go well with fern fronds?" Wade asked casually.

Wizzer nodded, straight-faced. "If you have a wine that's not pretentious."

"Come along, Muffin," Bronwynn said haughtily, unwilling to have her pet be the butt of any more jokes. "Let's go back to your pen."

"Closing the barn door after the horse has escaped?"

Wade asked. He picked up the tattered remains of the cigarette carton and raised an eyebrow.

Bronwynn shot him a look of annoyance. "I don't own a horse or a barn."

As she strode stiffly for the backyard with Muffin at her heels, Wizzer leaned against the looted car and laughed from his belly up. Wade's brows lowered, but the corner of his mouth quirked up in a reluctant smile. "Some day I'm going to send her to a class in remedial maxims."

"Well," Bronwynn said, forcing a smile while she fought against the reflex to gag. "They were certainly . . . unusual."

"Nnn," was the best response Wade could come up with. They had reached a truce over the sheep and car incident. Bronwynn had helped clean up the mess the animals had made on the upholstery of his car, and he had eaten fern fronds to make up for his nasty remarks about Muffin. He silently vowed never to say another word about that sheep for as long as he lived.

Bronwynn decided to give in to her true feelings. She pushed her plate away. "Uck. Yuck. They not only looked like something the cat coughed up, they tasted like it too. I'm sorry I made you eat them, Wade."

"Me too." He pushed his own plate away on the top of the work island and automatically reached to his pocket for a cigarette, then remembered the sheep had shredded them. Instead of feeling impatient, he decided he hadn't really wanted one anyway. Glancing around the kitchen he said, "This room is really shaping up, sweetheart. You're doing a great job."

A pleased flush bloomed on Bronwynn's cheeks. The kitchen was beginning to look new. The cupboards had been stripped and repainted white. The walls had been sanded and sized and now awaited the pretty wallpaper that was still in rolls on a table. Ugly linoleum had been removed, revealing a beautiful parquet floor that had required a good scraping and polishing. The room was coming to life with the promise of character and beauty. And Bronwynn had done much of the work herself—with help from Wade.

"I can't take all the credit," she said, reaching across the counter to twine her fingers with his.

"I provided a little muscle, that's all," Wade said, discounting his part. It really was Bronwynn's doing anyway. If not for her resolve, Foxfire would have been nothing but a memory by now. Looking around at the half-finished kitchen, seeing the potential charm and style of the room, he felt no regret for the abandoned ski lodge plan. His gaze landed back on Bronwynn. "I owe you an apology. If it hadn't been for your determination, this place would have slid the rest of the way into ruin. I misjudged you at first; I really didn't think you'd stick it out. You proved me wrong. I'm proud of you."

Her heart swelled with a warm full feeling again. It was love, wasn't it? Surely it had to be the real thing if four words like *I'm proud of you* could make her feel so happy.

Suddenly her nose began to twitch. She sniffed. "Do you smell something funny?"

"You mean besides new paint, polyurethane, and marinated fern fronds?" he asked dryly. "No. What do you smell?"

Bronwynn sniffed again, puzzled. "I'm not sure—"

A racket in the front yard intruded on the discussion. There was the crunch of tires on gravel as a car drove in. Tucker barked tiredly from the porch, in accompaniment to the unmistakable sound of a sheep bleating.

"Sounds like company," Wade said as they headed down the hall to the front door. "Too bad they didn't get here sooner; we could have foisted fern fronds off on them."

Bronwynn stepped out onto the porch and her smile froze on her face. Parked in front of her steps was a gunmetal gray Jaguar. Muffin had somehow managed to escape her pen and now stood with her front feet on the driver's door of the car, staring directly into the face of Ross Hilliard.

A frown creased Wade's forehead as he watched the driver emerge from the passenger's side of the car. The man was tall with meticulously combed dark hair and expensively tailored clothes. He wore a petulant frown as easily as he wore his Canali original raw silk jacket.

"Do you know him?" Wade asked Bronwynn, who stood at attention beside him like a Doberman ready to attack.

"Oh, yes, I know him," she said sharply, never taking her eyes off Ross's face. "That's the creep I almost married."

Muffin bounded up the steps ahead of Ross and stood at the top bleating at him as if she fancied herself to be a guard dog. Ross scowled at the sheep. Muffin sniffed at him and stamped her feet.

"Bronwynn, what is this creature doing running around loose?" he asked in a Boston Brahman accent that was as dry as a good martini.

Bronwynn lifted her nose. It might have been dusted with freckles, but it was still patrician, and the gesture of icy disdain was unmistakable. "Muffin is my pet; she may run where she chooses. *She* belongs here. What's your excuse?"

"Your sister expressed a certain amount of concern over your determination to stay away from home. Naturally I felt compelled to check up on you."

"Get off it, Ross." His explanation was so absurd, she almost laughed out loud. "About the only thing Zane would express to you would be a swift kick. What did you do, sneak through her mail to find out I was up here?"

"I refuse to dignify your question with an answer."

She had to give him points for having mastered a hurt look. Not many people would have noticed the impatient lines that tightened ever so slightly around his mouth.

"Compelled to check up on me, were you? How thoughtful—nearly a month after the fact. What happened, Ross? Did Belinda get bored with you and run off with the tennis pro to Mazatlán?"

"You're hardly the one who should be slinging barbs, darling." He fixed his pale green stare on Wade but spoke to Bronwynn, anger accenting his speech. "Obviously the muck-raking press knew what they were talking about when they suggested you'd run off with another man. How long has this little affair been going on?"

Outrage made her pull her fists out of the pockets of her shorts. The urge to go for his throat was overwhelming. "You philandering pig! How dare you accuse me of running off with someone else, when you were panting after my own cousin behind my back. What were the two of you planning, Ross? Draining my trust fund, then a tidy divorce, or was I going to have an unfortunate accident on our honeymoon?"

"Really, Bronwynn," he said with a huff. "You completely misinterpreted my relationship with Belinda. I could have explained everything. In fact, I came here to do just that. However, I can see now that you were only looking for an excuse to leave me at the altar so you could dash off with this common Casanova."

Bronwynn was ready to start swinging. People may have questioned her sanity from time to time, but no one ever questioned her integrity. To have Ross do so was more of an insult than she could stand. While she was busy deciding where to hit him first, Wade stepped in front of her.

A red haze clouding his vision, he grabbed Ross Hilliard by his overstarched collar and backed him toward the steps. Never in his life had he felt such rage. The overbearing ass had hurt Bronwynn, and now he had the gall to be angry with her! Wade wanted to turn him inside out.

"I think you'd better leave, pal," he said tightly.

In spite of his pallor, Ross tried to brazen it out. "Or what? You'll break my nose?"

"Actually I had something nastier in mind, but I'd rather not waste my energy on a worm like you." With a little shove, he sent Ross stumbling down the steps. "For the record: Bronwynn didn't come up here to be with me. She came up here to get away from you. Devious bastard that you are, you would manage to read something suspicious into it. You're not trustworthy, so how can you expect anyone else to be? Bronwynn wasn't cheating on you. You're the one who blew it, Hilliard. Be a man and face up to your mistake instead of trying to blame someone else."

In the fading twilight, Ross looked very much like a sulky little boy, Bronwynn thought. How could she ever have believed she wanted to spend the rest of her life with him? It made her skin crawl to think of it.

"It would have served you right if I had run off with Wade," she said. "But I wouldn't stoop to your level. I couldn't get that low if I were run over by a steamroller. And for your information, Wade is hardly a common Casanova. He's a congressman."

"Bully for you," Ross said snidely.

Bronwynn tried to tamp down the urge to dismember him with her bare hands. "I'll ask you to leave now, Ross."

"You haven't heard the last of me, Bronwynn," he

said in warning, jerking his tie straight. "I won't take public humiliation lying down."

"Really?" She arched a delicate brow above her blue eye. "I would have thought that your favorite position."

"How amusing," he said with a sneer.

"Just so you don't have an excuse to come back here and harass me, I'll give you back your suitcase." She ducked inside the front door and returned from the hall closet dragging Ross's ruined bag. She heaved it down the steps, stood back, and dusted her palms. "I want you out of my life, bag and luggage."

"Baggage," Wade murmured under his breath. A broad grin took command of his mouth as he watched Ross's face when the man looked at the expensive case and clothing Bronwynn had set ablaze.

"What—what have you done?" Ross asked, sputtering as he peered through the hole in the top of the bag. Slowly he pulled a custom-tailored shirt out and stared, aghast at what was left of it. Ross lifted his gaze to glare at Bronwynn. "My luggage. My clothes. How could you?"

"You've heard of being burned in effigy?" Bronwynn said. "Think of this as being burned in Gucci."

"Can you believe the nerve of that man?" Bronwynn demanded, fuming as she paced the length of the parlor. She jammed her hands on her hips, then crossed her arms over her chest, then dragged her hands through her hair. "Thought he could come up here and worm his way back into my good graces. Accuses *me* of humiliating *him*! Boy, that's rich. Arrogant, obnoxious . . . argh!"

Wade stood at the end of the new rose sofa and watched her, his temper cooling slowly. "He didn't win any points for charm in my book. Why did you ever get hooked up with him, Bronwynn? If you were looking for a relationship like the one your parents had, I can't believe you thought you'd find it with him. He's the last man—"

He broke off as Bronwynn stopped and stood stock-still in the center of the room. He could almost hear the wheels turning in her mind as she tried to fit the puzzle pieces together.

Bronwynn scarcely dared breathe. She had caught the end of the thread that had eluded her, the one that would weave everything together. If she had been looking for a relationship like her parents had had . . . she wouldn't have chosen Ross. Why had she chosen him?

Wanting desperately to help her sort it all out, Wade thought back to the day she'd told him about her parents. He could still see the haunted look in her eyes when she'd spoken of her mother letting go of life after the car crash that had killed her husband. He went to Bronwynn and rested his hands on her shoulders. "Ross was safe—"

"Because I knew I would never love him so much that he could destroy me," she said softly, melancholy seeping through her. "Isn't it strange how perfectly clear it all is now?" She closed her eyes and stepped into his embrace, resting her cheek against his chest. "Oh, Wade, what a terrible mistake I would have made for me and for Ross. What an insult it would have been to my parents. What they had together was so wonderful."

He stroked a hand over her hair. "So wonderful it was frightening. You were protecting yourself, honey."

Protecting herself from love. It wasn't the way she wanted to live her life. It was better to live a short time with the kind of love that was deep and real than to live forever without it. Looking back on the last year, she could see it had been pale and passionless. She had been safe, but she hadn't been alive, not in the way she had been since she'd come to Foxfire—since she'd met Wade.

Everything was in focus now—not just her past, but her present as well. And the future wasn't just something she would drift aimlessly into. She could see what she wanted with startling clarity. It all began with the man before her. She wasn't positive of his feelings, but she was sure of her own.

Slowly she lifted her head to gaze up at Wade. "Wade, I—" Suddenly she sniffed, her brows knitting in concern. "There's that smell again. It's kind of musty and acrid and it sort of smells like—"

Wade's eyes went wide with realization. "Smoke!"

Nine

There was water everywhere. It dripped from the ruined kitchen ceiling, ran down the wall that had been
so carefully prepared to receive the new wallpaper—the
new wallpaper that was sitting on the table in a puddle
of water. Another thin puddle spread from the west
outer wall about halfway into the kitchen, seeping into
the parquet floor.

Bronwynn stood in the back doorway and surveyed
the damage with a look of shock. She knew the room
directly above the kitchen looked even worse, but she
didn't really care about that room. It was a small guest
bedroom she hadn't been planning to work on for a
long time. The kitchen was the room that now made
big tears swim in her smoke-stung eyes. She'd worked
so hard in here—she and Wade.

A layer of grimy soot coated the once-pristine white
cupboards and clung to the freshly sanded and sized
walls. It dusted the abandoned dinner dishes and the
food wrappers sitting on the work island, nearly oblit-
erating the logo on a fresh box of Twinkies. It ran in
muddy streaks down the outer wall.

While the water damage was limited to two rooms,

the smoke had reached every corner of the house. It was even in the closets, Bronwynn thought dejectedly. Everything she had scrubbed and polished over the past few weeks would have to be scrubbed and polished again. Every floor, every wall, every ceiling, every pane of glass in the thirty-seven windows.

Not all the damage had been caused by the fire. The overzealous firemen had gone axe crazy on the back screen door. The thing hung drunkenly from one hinge, kindling held together by shreds of wire mesh. Upstairs there was a gaping hole in what had been the bedroom wall.

"Pretty simple to figure out," the chief of the Shirley volunteer fire department said in an unusually cheerful voice. A small man with a round face and neatly trimmed black mustache, it appeared he was being swallowed whole by his brilliant yellow fireman's coat. His hat was too large and wobbled on his head as he spoke, making Bronwynn think of those toy ball players with the big bobbing heads her nephew collected. "Pete was using a torch on the outside trim today. The heat started the squirrel's nest in the upstairs wall to smoldering, the fire spread through the wall. If you hadn't caught it when you did, we could have had a doozy of a blaze out here tonight."

"We smelled smoke," Bronwynn murmured hoarsely. What had been a vague aroma earlier in the evening was now a thick stench that burned her nostrils and throat. She had heard someone in the large curious crowd that had gathered on her lawn say that smell would permeate everything in the house—draperies, clothing, her new sofa.

"I'm so sorry, honey," Wade said. He stood behind her with his hands on her shoulders. She felt thin and frail to him as she took a shuddering breath.

"First Ross, now this." Bronwynn turned and looked up at him, not that she could see him through the tears pooled in her eyes. Her lower lip trembled threateningly. "I'm not having a very good night."

"Oh, poor baby." Wade wrapped his arms around her as she fell, sobbing against his chest. There was a lump in his throat the size of Rhode Island. Trying to be gentle, he dragged her out the back door into the yard. She had gone corpselike in his arms and made no attempt to move her feet. "Come on, sweetheart. Let's get some fresh air."

The Green Mountain night air was cool and cleansing. Stars made diamond points of light in the black velvet sky. Now that the possibility of danger had passed and the fire was out, there was almost a party atmosphere in the yard. The firemen and the citizens of Shirley who had followed them up milled around, talking. Someone had a radio going. Someone else had brought a cooler of beer along. Muffin and Tucker worked their way through the crowd, looking for handouts.

Wade helped Bronwynn up to sit on the bed of her pickup, then sat beside her with his arm around her shoulders. "It'll be all right, honey. We'll get the mess cleaned up in no time. Pete told me he felt so bad about his torch being the start of all this, he's going to do all the repairs to the walls right away."

All Bronwynn could manage to do was sniffle pathetically. She was exhausted from the events of the evening. She had reached the end of her rope and was too tired, emotionally and physically, to dig her fingernails into the knot and hang on.

"Have a brownie, dearie," one woman offered sympathetically. She had a Roman nose and was built like a Marine, but her eyes were soft and kind. "Rose Lubonovich, " she said in introduction, then lifted the brownie pan. "They have caramel in them."

Bronwynn turned her head into Wade's shoulder and began to cry. Everyone was being so nice, she didn't think she could stand it much longer. She was trying so hard to be strong, but it was darn near impossible with everyone offering her their support. She wanted to sob until she melted down into a puddle like the one that was ruining her beautiful parquet floor in her charbroiled kitchen.

"I guess she don't like caramel," Rose said to Wade.

"I think she's just a little overwhelmed by it all," Wade said, stroking a soothing hand over Bronwynn's hair.

"Oh, yeah, I don't blame her a bit. You like caramel?"

He took a brownie to pacify Mrs. Lubonovich, then tossed it to Tucker after the woman had left. Kissing the top of Bronwynn's head, he worked his handkerchief out of his hip pocket and offered it to her. "At least I'm prepared this time. I don't have to rip your underwear."

A watery chuckle escaped Bronwynn as she recalled the first time she'd met Wade, how he'd held her while she'd cried, and how he'd torn her slip so she could have a hankie. "You're so sweet. You're always right here when I need you. I think you're the sweetest man alive, even if you do act like a porcupine half the time."

Looking embarrassed, Wade changed the subject. "I think it would be a great idea for us to get away for a few days. You don't really want to wash all those windows again. We can go somewhere while someone else deals with this mess."

"Go somewhere?" she asked, raking her hair back out of her eyes. "On a minivacation? What about all that paperwork you keep making noises about?"

Wade shrugged and wiped a smudge of soot off her chin. "It's not as important as you are."

Touched beyond words, Bronwynn leaned up and kissed his cheek. She knew how seriously Wade took his career. If he was willing to put her ahead of it, it had to mean he had strong feelings for her. She had been on the brink of telling him she was in love with him when the fire had broken out. She wanted to tell him now, but her emotions were running so high and her strength so low, she was certain she couldn't get through it without bursting into tears again.

Poor Wade had endured enough tonight. The last thing he needed was to have to sit through a profession of love delivered by a bawling woman who looked like a war refugee and smelled like a flame-broiled burger.

"Where do you want to go?" Wade asked, envisioning luxury accommodations, room service, and a Do Not Disturb sign. "Lake Champlain?"

Without the slightest hesitation Bronwynn said, "Camping."

"Camping?" His voice was flat and unenthusiastic.

"Camping."

"I had to be a sucker and give you a choice," he said dryly. Camping with Bronwynn? Bronwynn set loose in the woods? He'd written the script for another disaster. On the other hand, the idea of having her totally to himself in the wilds definitely held a primitive appeal. Visions of afternoons spent swimming naked with her in some clear mountain lake, and evenings spent slowly making love between the flannel folds of a sleeping bag ran through his head. "Okay, camping it is. Tonight you'll stay at my place."

"No argument," she said wearily, resting her head on his shoulder.

"You can take a long hot bath," he said, then sniffed her hair. "In fact, I insist on it."

Bronwynn managed to chuckle and elbowed his ribs.

Once the fire truck headed back into Shirley, the party broke up quickly. Mrs. Lubonovich left half a pan of brownies. Someone offered Bronwynn a thermos of hot coffee and the name of a professional cleaning service. Eventually the last of the neighbors drove away, taillights glowing red off into the quiet summer night.

Wade and Bronwynn sat on the pickup and watched as the dynamic duo of the raccoon world scampered into the kitchen through the tattered remains of the screen door.

Bronwynn sighed. "I'm too beat to chase them out."

"There's nothing left in there that's fit to eat anyway." He gave her shoulders a squeeze and winked at her. "Maybe they'll discover the last of Wizzer's fern fronds. That'll cure them from going into the house. They'll probably move to New Hampshire."

They slid down off the truck and started for the front of the house where Wade's car was parked. Bronwynn leaned against him, feeling safe and protected with his arm around her, her hip brushing his as they walked.

How would she have gotten through this night if it hadn't been for Wade? She knew she would have gotten through the confrontation with Ross. She would have survived the fire. Experience had taught her that her strength ran deep. But it would have been an even bleaker evening if not for the man beside her. She felt as though the rug had been yanked from under her feet. Wade had caught her when she would have fallen hard. He had offered strength when hers had run out. He'd given her a hankie when she had needed to cry.

Wade Grayson was some kind of guy. Unless she was way off the mark, he was *the* guy.

"Are you out of your mind?" Wade demanded to know.

Bronwynn blithely ignored the thundering scowl he wore. As he stomped around her, she sat on the living room floor, calmly and efficiently packing their backpacks with necessary supplies—extra socks, insect repellent, and three kinds of candy bars. She very discreetly slid Wade's carton of cigarettes under the sofa. "No. I'm a little unusual, but I'm perfectly sane."

He really didn't have to laugh to express his disbelief,

the look on his face said it all. Bronwynn paid no attention to him. Anyone would have thought by looking at her that her announcement had been perfectly reasonable, when, in reality, it was about as crazy as she was. Not for the first time Wade wondered how she could manage to exasperate him and arouse him all at once. No other woman he'd ever known would have suggested what Bronwynn had. He wanted to pick her up and shake her—then hug her and kiss her and take her back to bed and make love to her for the next month or so.

"You want to take that four-legged lint ball camping with us."

"I won't leave her here with strangers."

"Then leave her with the guy you got her from."

"Myron and Phyllis are in their RV on their way to a Knights of Columbus jamboree in Oswego, New York. Don't you keep up on anything that goes on around here, Wade?"

"Leave her with Wizzer."

"Forget it. Wizzer has a recipe for herbed mutton and new potatoes, remember?"

"Yes." Wade smiled unpleasantly. "I do."

"Muffin is going with us."

"What if we run across a bear? She'll be the first thing it goes for."

"Nice try. Wizzer told me there hasn't been a bear sighting around here in years. They're all farther north." She zipped the packs, stood up, and kissed Wade's cheek. He scowled at her again. She smiled, thinking he was unbelievably cute when he was being owly. "The only bear I'm likely to encounter on this camping trip is you, darling."

Wade ground his teeth as he watched Bronwynn carry the packs to the front door. The argument was pointless; he knew he'd give in. Still he had to admit he enjoyed sparring with her. It was fascinating to see how her completely skewed logic worked. "Bronwynn, you can't take a sheep camping."

"You're taking Tucker," she pointed out, carefully leaning her backpack so it wouldn't tip over.

"Tucker isn't a sheep. He's a dog. Dogs belong on camping trips."

Bronwynn made a face. "Oh, Wade, you're so traditional. Loosen up. If a dog can go camping, a sheep can go camping."

An hour later, they stood in the deep mountain forest—Wade, Bronwynn, and Tucker—staring at Muffin, who had managed to entangle herself inextricably in a stand of cockleburs.

"This," Wade said between his teeth, "is why you can't take a sheep camping."

Muffin was subsequently left in Wizzer's care after Bronwynn extracted a promise from the hermit that he wouldn't break out his recipe book. Wizzer gave them tea, directions, and some pastries made from the ground bark of birch trees. While Wade was poring over a hand-sketched map, Bronwynn took a neatly wrapped package from Wizzer and carefully tucked it away in her backpack.

It was afternoon by the time they made it to the spot Wizzer had told them about. It was exactly what Wade had pictured when he'd thought of having Bronwynn all to himself in the wilderness. Working together with quiet efficiency, they pitched their tent among the trees on the edge of a small meadow.

When the campsite had been set to rights, Wade wasted no time luring Bronwynn into the pool of clear cool water that was nothing more than a wide spot in a small, fast-flowing river. The beauty of the scene made his heart stop. The stream rushed down a wooded hill, tumbling over rocks, spilling in a spray of white over a ledge and into the pool. All around was the richness of the forest—the trees with their dark trunks and brilliant green foliage, ferns, tiny wildflowers of white, pink, yellow, and lavender. And the jewel in this setting was Bronwynn—so beautiful and uninhibited in her nakedness, she might have been a creature of the woods.

They splashed and played in the water, laughing like children. They made love under the spray of the tiny waterfall. Wade couldn't get enough of touching her, running his hands over her slick skin. She gave herself to him with no thought of reservation. She loved him. He would know that before they returned to civilization and the time for making decisions. For now, she reveled in Wade's lack of restraint, in the freedom of spirit that had seemed to be missing from his life when she'd first met him.

"What kind of candy bars do we get for supper?" Wade asked, teasing lights dancing in his eyes as he arranged wood for a camp fire.

Bronwynn shot him a look from where she sat on a log brushing her hair dry. "Supper was going to be the fish you didn't catch while we were making love."

"You expected me to catch fish while I was making love to you? That's kind of kinky, Bronwynn."

Rolling her eyes, she thrust his fishing pole into his hand. "Go see if you can get some trout to rise to your bait, Grayson. I refuse."

Wade kissed her nose and left camp whistling. Bronwynn watched him go, a warm smile of satisfaction curving her generous mouth. She looked at Tucker, who was sprawled on a bed of ferns.

"He's really coming around, Tucker," she said. "When I first met him he wouldn't have taken time to whistle, let alone go fishing."

The Labrador grumbled in his throat, obviously more interested in the cookies Bronwynn had dug out of her pack than in the important changes his master had undergone in the past few weeks.

The sun was sliding down over the mountain when Wade returned with their dinner—two small trout. He wasn't sure what he'd expected to find at the campsite upon his return, but it certainly wasn't a red plaid blanket spread beneath two place settings of gleaming white china and sparkling silver flatware.

"I didn't dare risk crystal," Bronwynn said, thrilled by the look on his face as he surveyed her handiwork. "We'll have to drink our wine from tin cups and pretend."

Speechless, his gaze fell on the bottle of white wine chilling in a container of water. The camp fire was burning—and nothing else. Bronwynn had wrapped two potatoes in aluminum foil and had them baking. She had gathered wild flowers and put them in a cup for a centerpiece. There was even a candle on their "table." The white taper was a little worse for wear, after spending the day in a backpack, but its crooked-ness only made it more endearing. Wade went to Bronwynn's pack and peeked inside.

"What? No evening gown?" Wade asked, teasing her gently.

Bronwynn dodged his gaze, fighting a secretive smile. She wore jeans and a baggy sweatshirt that hung nearly to her knees. "No. No evening gown."

They cooked their trout over the open fire and dined without interference from the dog, who had earlier been bribed with cheese sandwiches and now lay snooz-ing on the other side of the fire. When the meal was finished and the dishes done, Wade pressed a kiss to Bronwynn's lips.

"Thank you," he murmured, gazing into her eyes. "That was a very special dinner."

Bronwynn's heart jumped into her throat in nervous

anticipation of what was yet to come. "It isn't over," she said softly, lifting her hand to his cheek. "This whole night is going to be special."

Wade felt his stomach tighten with desire as Bronwynn stood up. She unfastened her jeans, dropped them, and stepped out of them. Slowly she lifted the hem of her sweat shirt, peeling it up her body, leaving a trail of shimmering peach silk in its wake. The shirt was tossed aside and forgotten as she stood in the light of the fire letting Wade look his fill.

Sheer lace cupped her high, firm breasts and ran in a seductive vee that ended in a point below her navel. The silk clung to her subtle curves, skimming the tops of her long legs. Without a word, she turned and went into their small tent.

When Wade stepped into the tent, his breath caught in his throat. A small battery-powered lantern glowed in one corner. The functional sleeping bags had been covered over with an ivory satin sheet, and Bronwynn lay stretched across it, looking up at him with undisguised desire.

Like a man in a trance, he unbuttoned and stripped off his shirt. His shoes and jeans followed. Not willing to take his eyes off the lady waiting for him, he struggled to deal with white cotton briefs that were snagged on the evidence of his passion.

Bronwynn came to him, eager to help, eager to drive him to madness with her hands. While she worked to free him, she ran her lips across the fevered skin of his tanned chest, her tongue flicking across the hard-knotted flesh of his nipples. Her mouth followed the line of dark hair down over the quivering plane of his belly and lower.

Wade wove his fingers into her fine hair, his trembling hand cupping the back of her head. He moaned aloud as she freed him from one prison and trapped him in a sweeter one.

He lifted her to him, kissing her deeply, running his hands over the silk of her nightgown as they kneeled together on the thick cushion of their bed. Through the film of lace, he teased her swelling breasts. His fingers followed the vee down across her stomach.

Bronwynn gasped into his mouth as his hand trailed lower, pressing the cool silk between her thighs as his fingers found her most sensitive flesh. Her hips danced to the tune his hand played. He bent her back over his arm and closed his lips on the sensitive peak of her breast, sucking strongly at her through the barrier of lace. An explosion of sensation rocketed through her as her passion crested.

She called his name as she stiffened in his arms. As he lowered her to the sheet, she told him she loved him. She murmured it over and over as she took him in her arms, chanted it as she took him deep inside her, cried it out as he took her over the edge again.

Outside the tent, night's blackness had given way to the soft dark gray of early morning. Bronwynn lay awake, studying Wade's face in sleep. He looked younger, relaxed in a way he never could be when he was conscious. Even though she'd seen him slowly unwinding over the last few weeks, Bronwynn didn't fool herself into thinking Wade would ever become laid-back. He was a doer, a worrier, a man who was committed to ideals and beliefs that demanded almost constant attention. That was part of what she loved about him, she supposed. She admired his conviction, yet she was able to see his need for lightness and fun in his life, his need for someone to care for him as a man.

She loved him. During the long night of passion she had told him in every conceivable way that she loved him. Wade had responded with kisses, with caresses, but not with words. She shivered a little. She wasn't going to pretend she didn't need to hear the words. She knew Wade cared for her, but how deeply?

Was he convinced they were too different to ever have a future together? She didn't fit the mold of the politician's wife. Maybe he thought she'd hurt his image.

Immediately she scolded herself for having believed for a second that Wade was capable of being shallow. She knew he was a man of depth and character—even though she hadn't known him long.

Perhaps time was the reason Wade hadn't verbalized his feelings. Perhaps Wade felt it was too soon to make any kind of commitment. Unfortunately time wasn't on their side. He was leaving soon. If they didn't decide about their future now, it was going to be too easy for him to go back to his high-pressure career, to become immersed in it again, and forget about them.

Bronwynn wasn't willing to let that happen. One of the first things she'd decided when she'd come to Vermont was to take control of her life, to set goals and go after them instead of simply coasting through. She wasn't about to let Wade Grayson drift away from her. If he didn't bring up the subject of their future first, she was going to as soon as they got back.

She wouldn't quite admit to herself that she didn't want to bring up the subject of their future now. This camping trip was a special time. She didn't want it marred by a possible argument— especially not by one that could possibly end their relationship.

Shivers ran over her as she shoved the thought from her mind. She snuggled closer to Wade, realizing suddenly that the morning air was cool and crisp and she wasn't wearing much more than an afterglow. As she tried to burrow under him, Wade cracked one eye open and stared at her with a bemused expression.

"Bronwynn," he asked in a voice that was little more than a growl, "what are you doing?"

She nuzzled her nose in the curling hair at the base of his throat. "Trying to crawl under you. I'm cold."

At once Wade was wide awake. "Honey," he said, rolling on top of her and settling himself intimately in the cradle of her legs, "if you want to be beneath me, just say so."

His lips hadn't quite made it all the way to hers when the rain began. They heard it coming down through the trees before it landed, thunk, thunk, thunk on their tent. Not thirty seconds later a mournful howling began right outside the tent.

"Oh, Wade," Bronwynn said plaintively, instantly moved by Tucker's canine lamentation.

Wade's dark brows drew together above a frustrated frown. "He can crawl under a pine tree and stay perfectly dry."

Tucker's answer to that suggestion was another wail. Bronwynn looked up at Wade with her most eloquently pleading expression. Grumbling about being too blasted softhearted, Wade pulled his jeans on and let the dog in. Tucker ambled to the middle of the joined sleeping bags, shook himself all over Bronwynn, then proceeded to lay down and roll, drying himself on the ivory satin sheet.

Wade raised an eyebrow at Bronwynn's expression of dismay. "Happy now?"

The shower ended shortly after it had begun, but the sky refused to clear. The lack of sunshine had no effect on Bronwynn's and Wade's day, however. They explored the meadow and the woods around them, quietly walking hand in hand, enjoying each other's company and the beauty of the wild country.

Wade's gaze fell on Bronwynn more than it did on the scenery. He was in love with her. If he hadn't known it for certain before, he knew it now. He couldn't have begun to describe the soul-deep elation he'd felt in hearing the words from her. It had moved him. It had frightened him. He'd never been in love before. He was a man who seldom took a false step on his own turf, but he was on new ground and he wasn't at all sure of his footing.

Bronwynn loved him, but how strong were the ties that had only just begun to form between them? How much of what she felt was a need for stability after her relationship with Ross Hilliard had crashed and burned? Did she love him enough to leave Foxfire? If they'd had more time together, they could have strengthened the delicate thing between them, nurtured it. But he was going to have to leave soon. Was their love strong enough to survive outside the quiet cocoon of the Green Mountains?

She's such a free spirit, he thought as he watched her stare in fascinated awe at a doe with twin fawns that had ventured to the edge of the secluded meadow. Would she resent the lifestyle of a politician's wife? Would it stifle her? Or would she bring color and fun to it?

There was only one sure way to find out the answers to his questions. They were going to have to sit down and have a serious discussion. They'd talk as soon as they got back, he decided. That would give him enough time to get his arguments logically planned out in his head.

Two days later they broke camp reluctantly. Wade took care of the tent, Bronwynn repacked their backpacks, sneaking her gift from her pack into Wade's. She had it all figured out—they would go back to Wade's house with the gear they'd borrowed from Dr. Jameson's basement. While they were unpacking, Wade would discover the gift, then she would make her pitch for their continued relationship.

Butterflies swooped through her stomach. She'd never been one for designing strategies. It made her nervous to think that something might foul up her plan.

They picked Muffin up at Wizzer's and continued on their way back to civilization, content to carry on a desultory conversation as they walked hand in hand, each holding onto a leash on the other side. When they emerged from the woods in Bronwynn's backyard, she unsnapped Muffin's lead and let the sheep wander to a favorite grazing spot. Wade let his dog go and watched with amusement as Tucker followed the ewe and sprawled in the grass where he could keep an eye on her. As unlikely a pair as the two of them, Wade thought, glancing at Bronwynn.

"What's wrong?" he asked. Her expression was one of puzzlement, her gaze riveted on the house.

"Who are all those people?"

From where they stood, unnoticed at the back edge of the property, Wade counted at least a dozen people milling around on the lawn. He couldn't recognize any of them from a distance, but it was clear they weren't neighbors. Many of the men and women were dressed in business attire. Those who were in more casual clothes wore cameras around their necks. A sense of foreboding ran through Wade.

"The press," he muttered.

Suddenly one man turned and looked right at them. Then all hell broke loose.

Ten

It was a stampede. The media thundered across the lawn, photographers in sneakers overtaking reporters in dress shoes and heels. All of them were shouting at once, arms raised and waving. Mingled in with the noise of voices was the buzz and whirl of camera motor drives as pictures were snapped by the overeager paparazzi. Into the fray jumped Tucker and Muffin, barking and bleating and body slamming reporters. Before Bronwynn could fully comprehend what was going on, she found herself in the middle of the madness.

"Ms. Pierson, how long has this clandestine relationship with Congressman Grayson been going on?"

"Ms. Pierson, how long had you been planning to jilt Ross Hilliard?"

"Are you aware Congressman Grayson's constituents believe he's on a fact-finding mission in Rangoon?"

"Is it true Pierson's Chewing Gum is in line for a Pentagon contract?"

Bronwynn didn't have a chance to respond to any of the questions that came in rapid-fire succession. Stunned was a mild word for what she was feeling. She practically had grown up on the society page and always had been able to handle the press with ease, flashing them a smile and a glib remark, but now she was dumbfounded. They didn't belong here, not at Foxfire. It was her sanctuary. They were violating her special place of refuge. And worse than that, they were violating her relationship with Wade, making it sound tawdry.

What were they doing here? How had they found her? No one had known of her whereabouts except Zane . . . and Ross. Ross Hilliard, that filthy rotten louse, she thought. It wasn't bad enough that he nearly had ruined her life by marrying her, now he had to stoop to sicking the press on her as well.

As if they hadn't realized Bronwynn hadn't answered their rabid queries, the reporters turned on Wade, who was as flabbergasted as Bronwynn was.

"Congressman, did you ever have any intention of going to Rangoon? Was Ms. Pierson going with you?"

"Congressman, is this tryst being funded by the taxpayers?"

Wade's fierce scowl prompted another round of picture taking. Before he could open his mouth to respond to the insulting questions, Murphy Mitchell shoved his way to the front of the crowd.

The congressman's aide turned to face the media, blocking their view of Wade and Bronwynn with his stocky build and outstretched arms. He looked as if he'd been trampled in the race across the lawn. His tie was askew, and half the tail of his white shirt hung out of his grass-stained slacks.

"If you all will bear with us and be patient, Congressman Grayson and Ms. Pierson will have a formal statement to issue shortly."

"How shortly?" one reporter shouted.

"Long enough to get their stories straight?" asked another.

"There's nothing to get straight, ladies and gentlemen." Murphy said sharply. "This is all perfectly innocuous and very easy to explain. All we're asking for is a modicum of courtesy on your part. The press conference will be held on the front lawn in fifteen minutes."

Without another word to anyone, he hustled Wade and Bronwynn to the house, to the upstairs turret bedroom, where no one could listen in on their conversation.

"Murphy, what the hell is going on here?" Wade demanded, trying to keep his voice down as he helped Bronwynn remove her backpack, then shrugged out of his own.

Pacing back and forth across the dusty wood floor, Murphy ran a nervous hand over his thinning dark hair. He gave his boss an incredulous look. "What the hell is going on here? A zoo, that's what. A couple of days ago someone fed the press a juicy little story about the two of you. As you can see, no one wasted any time beating a path up here to check it out. I tried to explain the situation to them, but your rather conspicuous absence made them skeptical to say the least."

"This is all Ross's fault, Wade," Bronwynn said, crossing her arms. She felt at fault too. She'd had to shoot her mouth off and tell Ross who Wade was. It probably wouldn't have made any difference if she hadn't. She had been Ross's target in this nasty little scheme, it wouldn't have mattered whom she'd been with. "Petty bastard. He swore revenge, you'll remember."

"Too well." Wade turned to Murphy. "What did you tell them?"

"The truth," Murphy said earnestly. "That you came up here for health reasons, that Ms. Pierson's presence was merely coincidence. I explained to them that your relationship with Ms. Pierson was strictly business, concerning the purchase of her property here in Vermont."

Bronwynn felt as if she'd taken a blow to the chest. She stared at the man, too stunned to move. Purchase of property? Strictly business? Murphy obviously believed every word he was saying. He had no reason to lie. How would he have gotten the impression he had, unless it was what Wade had told him? The guilty look on Wade's face told her all she didn't want to know.

Murphy went on, oblivious to the undercurrents between the other two people in the room. "I told them you and I had discussed the possible purchase of this property several times over the phone. I even brought out the sketches we had done of the ski lodge we were planning to build."

How she managed to stay on her feet was a complete mystery to Bronwynn. She felt numb all over, inside and out. She watched Murphy turn to the carved mahogany bed, unzip an oversize portfolio. He withdrew several large pen-and-ink drawings of a modern ski lodge. She wondered vaguely if what she was feeling was anything like an out-of-body experience. As she stared at the draftsman's idea of what should be standing in place of her wonderful old house, she felt detached. If only what was happening was as unreal as it seemed, she thought.

With painful clarity she recalled every question Wade had asked her about Foxfire over the past few weeks. More than once he had asked her if she was considering selling. In fact, he had encouraged her to sell. From the first he had discouraged her from staying. As recently as two days ago he had asked her what her plans were.

She had hoped he'd been thinking about their future together then. Lord, what a fool she'd been. No wonder Wade hadn't told her he loved her. Their relationship had been a business matter to him with some fabulous sex thrown in as a fringe benefit. He had taken what had been freely offered. What man wouldn't have?

Men. She had come up here to escape one Machiavellian male and had entangled herself with another, telling herself once again that she was in love with him. How could she have been so stupid? She had known Ross for years and he had betrayed her. How could she have let herself trust Wade Grayson? She hadn't known the first thing about him. Was she so in need of love that she had to latch on to the first man to show her a little kindness after a heartbreaking experience?

Part of her still wanted to deny what Murphy was saying. She didn't like to think she'd been made a fool of twice in one summer. She didn't want to believe what she'd shared with Wade had been less than love. But Murphy Mitchell wasn't lying, and he was holding the proof in his hands, sketched in black and white.

"I tried telling them the two of you were about as mismatched as cheese and peaches," Murphy said with a half-laugh. "But they wouldn't believe me." He shook a finger at his boss. "I warned you about this, Wade. I told you they'd jump all over the sex angle—"

"Murphy, shut up," Wade said through his teeth, his gaze locked on Bronwynn. He felt sick at the look on her face. Her thoughts played across it like a movie on a screen. She was taking everything Murphy said straight to heart and damning him straight to hell. He could feel the foundation of their very new and fragile relationship crumbling beneath his feet, and panic clenched like a fist in his gut. Reaching out to her he said, "Bronwynn, I can explain."

She jerked away from him, rubbing her arm where he'd touched her as if he'd burned her. Her chin trembled ever so slightly, but she stood as straight and stiff as a post. If she couldn't salvage anything else out of this mess, at least she could cling to her pride. "There's no need, Wade. Your henchman has done a more than adequate job."

"Henchman?" Murphy protested.

Wade waved him off, his gaze locked on Bronwynn. "Bronwynn, if you would just listen—"

"I'll listen," she said, crossing her arms over her chest, as much to hide the trembling in her limbs as to take a belligerent stance. "You tell me—did you ever have any intention of buying this property to build a ski lodge on?"

Wade's heart sank even further. If she didn't let him explain, his answer was going to drive the final nail into the coffin lid. He never had mentioned his former plan for buying the property because he had given it up as soon as he'd seen how important Foxfire was to Bronwynn—and how important Bronwynn was to him. But would she believe him even if she gave him the chance to explain? He had a sick feeling the answer to the question was no.

"Yes," he said, forcing the word out of his mouth, "but—"

She winced as if he'd struck her. Staring down at the wood floor to hide the tears that pooled in her eyes, quietly she said, "That's all I needed to hear."

As she turned to leave the room, Wade caught her arm, his fingers biting into the soft flesh. His eyes were pleading, his voice was rough and smoky with the need for understanding. "Bronwynn, it's not at all what you're thinking."

"That you used me? That I was the recreation part of your R and R trip to Vermont? That you heard my story and thought 'Oh, great. Here's a little fool I can have some summer fun with'?"

Frustrated that he couldn't will her to listen to him, Wade pulled her closer to him. "You're a little fool, all right. Bronwynn, I love you."

She glared at his hand on her arm, then raised her gaze to his face, her mismatched eyes blazing like jewels. "What a convenient time to say so." Bitterness coiled like a snake inside her. "Don't worry, Congressman, I won't tell the press what a bastard you are. After all," she said mockingly, "this situation is perfectly innocuous and easily explained. It was strictly business. Too bad nobody bothered to tell me."

She played the press with a cunning that was almost ruthless, Wade thought as he listened to Bronwynn answer questions and turn accusations around. His Bronwynn, who was always so laid-back, could be a tigress when she was cornered.

His Bronwynn. She wasn't his anymore. She had been quick to believe the worst of him, and Wade had to wonder if she ever had been his. He hurt on two different levels. He couldn't stand to have his integrity questioned. He was and always had been scrupulously honest—to have anyone think differently was the worst kind of affront. But he found the deepest hurt was that she questioned his love.

He hadn't told her soon enough that he was in love with her, but then, he'd never been in love before. It was new to him. So far, he wasn't wild about the experience. First he had to go and fall for a woman who drove him bonkers, who was his opposite in every way. Now he hurt right down to his toenails, because Bronwynn had taken his declaration of love and spit it right back in his face.

Dammit, how could she lose faith in him so quickly? How could she believe he was capable of such duplicity? Well, he'd known all along the workings of her mind were a mystery worthy of Sherlock Holmes. The woman didn't know what logic was. Steer clear of her, he'd told himself right from the start. Why hadn't he taken his own advice?

"How do you explain the backpacks you were wearing when you came out of the woods, Ms. Pierson?" asked one of the reporters who was standing at the foot of the porch.

"There are nearly three hundred and fifty acres of

forestland on this property," Bronwynn explained coolly, looking down her nose at the woman. She was discovering anew the depth of her strength. She ached to find a quiet, private corner to curl up and suffer in, but she'd be damned if she'd let either the press or Wade see how badly she was hurting. "Congressman Grayson and I were going over it to determine if it would be suitable for cross-country ski trails."

"And are you going to purchase the property, Congressman?" questioned a young field reporter from one of the major television networks.

"No," Wade said quietly.

Bronwynn jumped in before he could say more. "We were unable to come to terms. I've decided to keep Foxfire, renovate the house and grounds, and open it as a bed and breakfast inn."

"Then you won't be going back to Indiana with the congressman?"

He never invited me, she thought, pain slicing through her. *Damn you, Wade Grayson, for making me fall in love with you. Damn me for being fool enough to do it.* "No, I won't be going to Indiana." She shot a look at Wade, her eyes full of accusation. "I was never going to Indiana."

"What do you have to say, Congressman?"

Wade's level gaze never left Bronwynn's face. The stubborn set of his jaw, the line of his mouth betrayed his inner pain, but neither was something the gossip hounds noticed. In general he appeared relaxed, bored even. His tone of voice was sardonic. "Our department of tourism will be disappointed."

"How does Ross Hilliard figure into this scenario, Ms. Pierson?"

Bronwynn saw red at the mention of Ross's name. He had sworn to get revenge on her for walking out on their wedding. He was getting revenge all right, the rotten creep. There hadn't been a method of torture yet invented that was hideous enough for use on him, but she was thinking up several that came close.

She managed an indolent shrug and raised a questioning brow at the reporter. "You tell me. As far as I'm concerned, Ross Hilliard is ancient history, water over the bridge."

"Under the bridge," Wade muttered, rolling his eyes.

Bronwynn wheeled on him, no longer able to hold back her temper. The wall she had hastily erected to keep in her emotions cracked then virtually exploded. "Dammit, will you stop correcting me! It can be water over the bridge if I want it to be!"

"No, it can't, because your bridge doesn't connect on both sides," Wade said, venting some of his own pent-up frustration. It wasn't like him to lose his cool in front of the press, but then he hadn't been himself since he'd met Bronwynn Prescott Pierson. Now he couldn't think about the reporters on the lawn. All he could think about was that he had given Bronwynn the privilege of being the only woman he'd ever fallen in love with, and she was treating him as if he were something that had just crawled out from under a rock.

"How dare you say such a thing to me you—you—you—man!" The word had become a curse to her once more. She turned to grab the sketches of the infamous ski lodge, intent on throwing them in Wade's face, only to find Muffin had snatched them from Murphy and was making a snack of them. Camera lenses zoomed in on the sheep. Muffin bleated and bolted off the porch, dashing around the side of the house. Frustrated, Bronwynn grabbed Murphy's portfolio and smacked Wade across the chest with it. "You can just take your ski lodge and stick it in your . . . home state. I wish I'd never laid eyes on you!"

"Believe me, lady, it's mutual," Wade said between his teeth.

Bronwynn stuck her tongue out at him, turned on

her heel, and stormed into the house, not remembering or caring that there was a mob on her front lawn—a mob that had recorded every word she'd said for the evening news, the morning papers, and the weekly tabloids. Wade stomped down the porch steps and made a beeline for his car. Murphy hurried along behind him, toting Wade's backpack. The reporters parted like the Red Sea lest they be mowed down, but they still shouted questions.

"Congressman, will you build the lodge in Indiana?"

"Did that bridge business have anything to do with the Safe Highways bill?"

"Congressman Grayson, does this mean your relationship with Ms. Pierson is over?"

Wade turned with one hand on the open door of his Lincoln and one braced on the roof. His eyes were trained on the door of the big old Victorian house. Pain dug its talons into him.

"Absolutely," he said tightly. He glanced at the reporters and flashed them a pale shadow of his famous smile. "Feel free to quote me on that."

" 'The Congressman and the Coquette: Land Deal or Liaison of Love?' " Zane read the tabloid headline aloud. She had arrived on the scene too late to protect her baby sister from the press, but not too late to offer a shoulder to cry on.

"*Coquette*?" Bronwynn said, making a face. "Uck!" She leaned her elbows on the kitchen work island, which also served as breakfast bar, and stared down at her untouched Twinkie and the plate of scrambled eggs her mother-hen sister had plunked down in front of her earlier.

Wizzer lifted another of the gossip rags Ross Hilliard had sent by special delivery. " 'Eccentric Heiress and Conservative Congressman—Moonlight in Vermont.' The

National Inquisitor calls it 'a sizzling summer sex scandal.' "

Bronwynn groaned. In the back of her mind she worried what the headlines were doing to Wade's career, then she scolded herself for caring. He'd taken the worst kind of advantage of her. What did she care if his conservative constituents back in Indiana wanted to string him up by his thumbs. They were the least of what she wanted to string him up by.

Zane reached across the table to pat her sister's hand reassuringly. "It's all over now, honey. With neither you nor that cad congressman making any statements to the press, the hoopla will die down in a matter of days. Just be thankful you found him out and got rid of him before it was too late. I knew he was trouble the minute I set eyes on him."

Wizzer laughed. He seemed enormously amused by the whole thing. "You caught them in a clinch, too, huh?"

Zane lifted her slim nose haughtily. "I beg your pardon?"

"I don't want to talk about it," Bronwynn said, propping her chin on her hand. She stared morosely at her new screen door and the two raccoons that sat on the other side staring in.

"That's all right, sweetheart," Zane said with a sympathetic look. "It's best to put it all behind you. Forget about the man. He was an unscrupulous cretin."

"Rabbit raisins!" Wizzer bellowed, spreading a liberal layer of grape jelly on an English muffin. "You blew it, Red."

Zane bristled. "How dare you speak that way to my sister!"

Wizzer snorted. "I'm an old hermit, I can say what I want." He took a huge bite of his muffin then carefully wiped the grape jelly out of his mustache. His blue eyes were like lasers when he turned them on Bronwynn. "Use your noodle, Red."

"Wizzer, he took advantage of me," Bronwynn said defensively. It was really quite remarkable how fresh the pain felt every time she thought of what had happened.

"How?"

Bronwynn blushed. "He knew I was vulnerable . . ."

"And?"

And he took everything I had to offer him, then he hurt me and walked away. Unfortunately for her conscience, her memory wasn't capable of being selective. Other images of her time with Wade surfaced as well. *And he held me when I cried and listened when I needed to talk.*

Guilt nipped at her with sharp little teeth, not for the first time since the big blowout two days before. Her sense of righteous indignation bit right back when she thought of the sketches of the would-be ski lodge. "All he ever wanted was Foxfire."

First Ross had wanted her for her money, then Wade had wanted her for her land. It stung like the dickens to think neither had wanted her for herself.

"Bullfrogs," Wizzer said, pouring himself another cup of tea.

Zane nibbled on her toast with a disapproving frown. "The man was obviously devious. He wasted no time making contact with Bronwynn, trying to take advantage of her emotional state—"

"He stayed here that first night because he was worried about me," Bronwynn said, bewildered by her need to defend the man who had betrayed her.

"—and forced his company on her continually after that—"

"Actually," Bronwynn interjected, thinking of how often she had intruded on Wade's privacy in an attempt to lure him away from his work, "it was more the other way around."

Zane's black brows pulled together in annoyance as

she turned her gaze on her sister. "Just whose side are you on?"

Wizzer lifted a bushy brow and waited for her answer. Bronwynn squirmed on her stool, wrestling with the question inside her. She frowned at her hermit friend. "Why didn't he ever tell me about the ski lodge?"

"Maybe because it wasn't important to him anymore."

"But the sketches—"

"Don't prove donkey doodle. Maybe he was interested in the land once. Are women the only ones who are allowed to change their minds?"

"No, but Murphy—"

"Obviously didn't know the whole story. Did you give College Boy a chance to explain, Red?"

Wade had told her he could explain, but she'd been too hurt to let him. He could have set things right at the press conference. Had he been too hurt to try again? Not only had she questioned his love, she had questioned his integrity as well. She remembered how furious she had been when Ross had wrongly accused her. How must Wade have felt when she had done the same thing?

If he was indeed innocent. Bronwynn still felt safer clinging to her pain than believing in him.

"Open your eyes, Red," Wizzer said, gesturing to their surroundings with his English muffin. "Look around you. How many hours did the two of you spend working on this house? Why would he if he was planning to buy the property? Why would he spend his vacation time helping drive up the value of this place if he wanted to buy it and bulldoze the house? You think he's a moron?"

"No," Bronwynn said softly, feeling properly chastened. She looked around the kitchen. The soot had been scrubbed away, the water cleaned up, the floor polished. She didn't need to coax the memories of Wade helping her in the room to have them come to the surface. He had helped her sand and size the walls. He had helped her pull up the ugly carpet. Color rose in her cheeks as she remembered the day they had steamed the old wallpaper off the walls and had ended up on the floor beneath the stuff.

He might have helped her just to get into her good graces, she thought. Maybe he had done it as some kind of perverse private joke. Neither possibility seemed very likely. As hurt as Bronwynn was, she still couldn't believe he was a monster. In truth, beneath her hurt she couldn't think he was any kind of a monster at all.

Wade had the power to set her ablaze with a look or a touch. He had the tenderness to comfort her, the audacity to tease her. The only thing they had agreed on was their attraction to each other. She had known him only a few weeks, but he was no stranger. There had been a deeper sense of communication between them from the first. Now she felt ashamed for letting fear and distrust override her instincts.

Taking her Twinkie with her, Bronwynn slid off her stool. "Excuse me for a few minutes, will you?" she said to Zane and Wizzer. "I need to think."

She sat down on the back steps, glancing at Bob and Ray, who sat a discreet distance away, their eyes on her Twinkie. With a resigned sigh, she broke her Twinkie and tossed each half to a raccoon.

Wizzer was right, she had blown it. Ross's betrayal had left her wary, ripe to believe the worst of Wade. The evidence against him had been circumstantial, but damning to someone who so recently had been deceived. She simply had reacted to the situation instead of holding her pain at bay long enough to look at the facts. She had done him a terrible disservice. If only Wade had explained about the land deal earlier. If only they had had more time together to build trust. If only—

"If only's aren't going to solve this mess, are they,

Muffin?" she asked, rubbing the head of the sheep that had scaled the steps in search of attention.

What was she going to do? She loved Wade Grayson. Even when she'd believed he'd betrayed her, she had loved him. That was why it had hurt so very badly, far worse than Ross's deceit had. Only true, deep love had the power to cause such pain. She loved Wade the way she had always dreamed of loving someone—with every fiber of her body and soul. The thought of losing him was unbearable.

She loved Wade, but would he believe her after the way she'd treated him? She had accused him of some rotten things. Why should he take her back? In a moment of desperation he had told her he loved her, too, but had that fragile feeling been crushed by her lack of trust?

There was only one sure way to find out, she thought resolutely, swallowing down a major case of nerves. She had to go to Wade and ask him.

The old Bronwynn might have just waited to see if Wade would come back to her. The old Bronwynn would have drifted along with the tide and accepted whatever happened as her fate. But she wasn't the old Bronwynn anymore. She had vowed to take control of her life. She had made a mistake and she would rectify it. She loved Wade Grayson, wanted Wade Grayson, and she was going to do whatever she had to to get him back.

Eleven

Murphy Mitchell took one look at his boss and said defensively, "All you ever told me was that she was a pain in the—"

Wade held up a hand to cut him off. It was the first thing his aide had said to him every morning since their return from Vermont. "Good morning" and "Hello" had disappeared from the man's vocabulary entirely. Wade's head was pounding hard enough from his own arguments, he didn't need to hear Murphy's again. Leaning his elbows on the desk, he pinched the bridge of his nose between thumb and forefinger and sighed heavily. "I know, Murphy, I know."

"Polls today are running thirty-four percent for you, twenty-nine percent against. Eight percent thought you were the quarterback for the Minnesota Vikings, and the other twenty-nine percent want to know where in hell is Rangoon and what does it have to do with Indiana." Murphy poured himself a cup of coffee, checking his appearance in the reflection on the metal pot. "I'm losing my hair over this, Wade. I tried to warn you. Women like that are nothing but trouble."

"Women like what?" Wade bristled. He was still furious with Bronwynn for having doubted him, but it didn't mean Murphy was free to insult her.

Mitchell's heavy shoulders lifted. He fussed with the knot in his tie. "Women like Bronwynn Prescott Pierson. Rich bit—"

Wade cut him off with a flaming look. "Bronwynn isn't a 'woman like that.' Bronwynn isn't like anybody." How true, he thought! No one on earth had the power to exasperate him the way she did.

"Hey!" Murphy raised a hand in surrender. "I'm on your side, remember?"

"Then let's just drop it." Wade massaged his temples, counting the seconds until he could take some more aspirin. Twelve thousand six hundred, twelve thousand five hundred ninety-nine . . .

"I can understand if you're still hung up on her, Wade."

"Murphy." One word had never held so much menace.

"Okay." Mitchell wisely backed off the topic. He flipped open an appointment book on the desk and made a note. "I managed to put off your meeting with Lawrence Brockton until next week. Things will have cooled down a little by then." Murphy rolled his eyes as he spoke of one of Wade's biggest backers. "You know the man thinks politicians should be as celibate as priests. He's going to rake your butt over the coals, friend—"

"Dammit, Murphy," Wade said. His temper had worn as thin as old flannel in the days since the press had descended on him and Bronwynn. "I don't need another blasted lecture from you! I know what my obligations are. I know what mistakes I made. I sure as hell don't need you browbeating me with it all. Just leave the damn paperwork and get out."

Murphy stepped back, his mouth thinning at the dressing-down from his boss. He dropped a sheaf of file folders on the desk and said tightly, "Fine."

When the door to his office closed, Wade dropped his

head into his hands and raked his fingers back through his already-ravaged hair. He hurt too much himself to worry much about Murphy's feelings. In fact, he was having a devil of a time not blaming Murphy for part of his pain. Murphy had been the one to bring up the land deal, but the man had only been doing his job, after all, trying to protect his boss's reputation. And it wasn't Murphy's fault Wade never had told him about the situation between Bronwynn and himself.

Hell, how could he have apprised Murphy when he had only just figured out for himself that he was in love with the woman? He hadn't even told Bronwynn about it—not in time, at any rate. What a mess, he thought.

Picking up the tabloid he had snatched away from his secretary on his way into his office, he read the headline aloud. " 'Representative's Romantic Rendezvous Ruined: Fur Flies At Foxfire.' " The photograph showed Bronwynn sticking her tongue out at him.

As Murphy had pointed out with tedious regularity over the last week, they were the sex scandal of the year. It was going to take months to smooth all the feathers the headlines had ruffled.

Wade knew a politician's private life was not strictly his own, but still it irked him to have his put under a microscope, dissected, and twisted around. More than once over the past week he had been tempted to try to set the story straight, but Murphy had talked him out of it. History had proven the best way to deal with gossip was simply to ignore it. The fire would die out if no one added fuel to it.

Wondering when the fire in his belly would die out, Wade peeled the last antacid tablet from the roll on his desk, popped it in his mouth, and promptly dug another roll out of the box in his top drawer. The way things were going, soon he would have to look into buying the stuff wholesale. His stomach was boiling and churning inside like an acid pit. He hadn't had a decent meal in a week. Since his return to his office in Lafayette, his diet had consisted mainly of coffee, antacid tablets, scotch, and more antacid tablets. Food held no appeal. Neither did the cigarette he picked up and rolled between his fingers.

He was dying to light it up. He really was. But he couldn't. He hadn't smoked one single cigarette since leaving Vermont, even though his nerves were shot and practically screaming for nicotine. Tormenting himself, that's what he was doing. He was being perverse in the extreme. But, dammit, every time he picked up a cigarette he thought of Bronwynn—of how she would disapprove, of her subtle campaign to get him to cut down.

She could be extremely clever when she wanted to be. It had been days before he'd realized he hadn't been smoking nearly as much as usual—and that Bronwynn had been behind it, sneaking his cigarettes away, distracting him from the harmful habit. His renewed trouble with his ulcer had come as something of a shock after having gone several weeks without so much as looking at a bottle of antacid. The taste of the stuff—to which he had once been nearly immune—now came close to making him gag. Bronwynn was at the root of that too. She had seen to it he'd had decent meals. In her own quirky way she had looked after him as no one had in years.

A wry smile twisted Wade's mouth as he wondered how much of her haplessness with tools had been an act. Keeping busy at Foxfire, saving Bronwynn from what he considered imminent disaster, had kept him away from work and the worry that went along with it. Dr. Jameson himself couldn't have prescribed a better remedy for stress. He had unwound with Bronwynn, had relaxed, and had fun.

He had fallen in love with her, and she had hurt him. Oh, how she had hurt him. Giving her his heart had also given her the power to cut him deeply. The depth of his pain when she had doubted him had left him stunned, had left him both unable and unwilling to defend himself.

Now that he'd had some time to recover and think about it, he could see the mistakes he'd made. He should have told her at some point about the aborted ski lodge idea. He should have told her sooner that he loved her. He should have been more understanding of her reaction to his supposed betrayal—after what she'd been through with Hilliard, it had been natural. He should have made her believe in him. The way he'd behaved had only confirmed her suspicions that he was a bastard.

He wondered about what to do. Common sense tried to tell him to let go, to leave her alone. She was where she wanted to be, he was where he needed to be. She had Foxfire, he had his work. It had always been enough for him before.

As he ran his unlit cigarette back and forth across his lower lip, Wade cast a cursory glance at the files Murphy had tossed on his desk. Before Vermont, he would have dug into them with relish, he would have felt guilty ignoring them for even five minutes. Now he couldn't rouse enough interest to lift the covers on them. His career had been knocked into second place in his life, bested by a red-haired minx he had virtually nothing in common with.

It was true. They were as mismatched as Bronwynn's eyes, but still he loved her. Everything else in his life was going to be on hold until he either got Bronwynn back or exorcized her from his soul completely.

Somehow Wade didn't think the latter was going to be possible.

He opened the bottom right-hand drawer of his desk and lifted out the only thing of Bronwynn's he had other than memories. The kaleidoscope had been carefully wrapped and tucked into his backpack with the words "I love you" scrawled on the paper. The polished wood cylinder with shiny brass bands was unmistakably Wizzer Bralower's handiwork, but it wasn't the kilt-clad hermit Wade thought of when he lifted the toy to his eye and stared at the brilliant, beautiful patterns. He thought of Bronwynn. She had brought color and whimsy to a world made gray by work and responsibility. Now she was gone from his life, and he felt worse than dead.

Setting the kaleidoscope aside, he leaned forward and punched the button on his intercom. "Mrs. Griffin, would you please call the airline—"

The sound of his secretary's shrill voice on the other side of the office door brought Wade up short. "What is the meaning of this?" she shrieked. "Who do you people think you are? You can't come barging in here! Congressman Grayson is not available."

Wade was halfway out of his chair when the door burst open and a television camera crew bustled in. Reporters and photographers followed them, jostling each other for position as they crowded into the room.

"What's the meaning of this?" Wade demanded, echoing his secretary's words. Hadn't they intruded on his life enough in the past week? If the blasted press hadn't shown up when they had, he would have had a chance to talk over the future with Bronwynn and his life wouldn't be such a miserable hell.

"Congressman, is it true you've had no advance warning about this press conference?"

"Press? . . . Murphy!" Wade bellowed, anger overriding decorum. He raked the reporters with his scowl. "Who the hell let you people in here?"

"I did," Murphy said from the doorway, meeting his boss's baleful glare with a look that was a strangely familiar cross between irritation and resignation.

Wade was ready to launch into him when a voice from behind Murphy added, "At my request."

If he hadn't been braced against his desk, Wade was certain he would have keeled over at the sound of the voice. His knees actually turned rubbery. It was all he could do to keep his jaw from dropping when Murphy stepped aside and Bronwynn walked into the room.

He might not have recognized her on the street. Except for a recalcitrant tuft of bangs, her fly-away hair was slicked back into a neat ponytail. Ragged jeans and baggy T-shirt had been traded in for a pencil-slim beige skirt and a boxy, masculine-styled brown plaid blazer over a silk camisole top. Framing her almond-shaped eyes was an enormous pair of professor-style horn-rimmed glasses. Wade thought she was the most incredibly sexy thing he'd ever seen.

"Congressman," Bronwynn said in careful greeting when she reached Wade's desk. Her teeth nibbled nervously at her neatly painted lower lip.

If Wade was overjoyed at seeing her, he was doing a bang-up job of hiding it. He looked surprised and a little bit wary. Well, she couldn't blame him, but she had hoped for a smile at least. After the fight she'd had with Murphy Mitchell to get in she could have used some encouragement.

Wade cleared his throat and took the hand she offered across his desk. "Ms. Pierson," he said, then bit his tongue to keep from groaning at the feel of her flesh against his. Electricity hummed through him, reminding him that he'd lain awake night after night aching for her.

Bronwynn fought the urge to turn tail and run. At this point she was certain she was doomed to failure and public humiliation, even though she did have the advantage of surprise. Wade was a politician, and not one who had to have his every word phonetically spelled out for him by a speech writer either. He was very capable of thinking on his feet. Sweat trickled down between her breasts. He was going to flay her alive and leave her carcass for the press she had invited into his office.

"You have me at a loss," Wade said neutrally. She hadn't given anything away yet. He found himself hoping she wasn't still furious with him, hoping she hadn't taken a page out of Ross Hilliard's book and arranged some kind of revenge. "Would you care to explain all this?"

"Umm . . ." Shaking like a leaf, Bronwynn clutched at the leather folder that held her notes. She surprised herself by sounding remarkably calm when she answered. "Certainly. It occurred to me that the press has been misled on certain points concerning our relationship. I took the liberty of inviting them here today to set the record straight."

Wade's eyes searched hers for deeper answers. What he saw was hope, apology, and stark terror. Optimism ribboned through him. "I see. Well, yes, I would have to agree with you—the reports haven't been accurate at all, at least not concerning my feelings."

"Or mine," she added, praying she hadn't imagined the added meaning in his words. "If I can have a seat, I have a statement to make, and I would also like to ask you a few questions."

Wade motioned her to the conference table along the far wall of his office. Noisily the press rearranged themselves for the best view. Bronwynn took the seat Wade pulled out for her. She was never so glad of a place to sit down in her entire life. Another second standing in front of his desk, and she was certain she would have wilted like week-old celery.

As microphones were set up on the table, Wade took the chair beside Bronwynn's and looked at her expectantly, then glanced at the long, slender legs she crossed demurely over each other. Lord, but she was sexy in that outfit, he thought. His fingers itched to pull her glasses off and free her hair, to shove her businesslike suit jacket off her shoulders and cup her breasts through the fabric of the little slip of silk that was masquerading as a blouse.

With trembling fingers, Bronwynn opened her folder and glanced at the notes scribbled on the lavender legal pad. Straightening the glasses she wore merely for affect, she addressed the reporters, squinting into the bright lights the television people had set up.

"First of all, I would like to say that I did not go to Vermont with the intention of meeting Congressman Grayson. Prior to my arrival at Foxfire, I had no idea who he was." She couldn't quite nip back a little smile as she caught Wade's disgruntled scowl from the corner of her eye. "I went to Vermont because I needed to get away so I could get my life back in order. Until the day of our last press conference, I had no knowledge of the congressman's interest in my property."

The statement brought gasps and anxious murmurs from the reporters. At the back of the room, Murphy turned green and collapsed onto a chair. The noise from the press rose in a crescendo until Bronwynn spoke again.

"In retrospect, I believe he never mentioned it to me because he had changed his mind about wanting the land. Is that correct, Congressman?"

"Yes," Wade said, his gaze locked on Bronwynn. Only the most rigid self-control kept his smile from becoming an embarrassingly enormous grin. He was off the hook. It didn't matter that she had doubted him. All that mattered was she believed in him now and she was there within arm's reach. To the press he said, "I was initially interested in the Foxfire property, until I saw how important it was to Ms.—to Bronwynn. I didn't know her personally when I went, on my doctor's orders, to Vermont. I wasn't sure I wanted to get to know her after we met," he said, chuckling at her narrow-eyed look of outrage. "Gradually, I changed my mind."

"Why the subterfuge about the land deal then, Ms. Pierson?" one reporter asked.

"A misunderstanding," Bronwynn said, her eyes begging Wade's forgiveness, "and a terrible lack of trust on my part."

"And too much pride on mine," Wade said, equally sincere.

Bronwynn glanced down at her notes, trying to focus through a thin film of tears on her doodle of storm clouds and lightning. So far things were going better than she had dared hope, but it wasn't over yet. Taking a deep, steadying breath, she asked, "Would you say that what transpired between us was due to a lack of communication, Congressman?"

"Absolutely." He nodded, reining in the urge to reach out and touch her. He wanted her in his arms, his mouth on hers. That was their best form of communication as far as he was concerned.

"We both said some things we didn't mean. Wouldn't you agree?"

"Wholeheartedly, with one exception."

"I know," Bronwynn conceded with a sigh, her shoulders slumping beneath the padding of her jacket. "You were right. It *is* water *under* the bridge."

"No."

"Yes, it is," she said peevishly. He would have to pick now to split hairs, she thought.

"Will you listen for once?" Wade asked, caught between wanting to hug her and shake her. "I love you. I said the words that afternoon. I meant it."

While the press digested the information, Bronwynn sat staring up at Wade. For what seemed like an eternity, she couldn't move, couldn't speak, couldn't breathe. Oh, how she had wanted to hear him say he loved her— and how badly she needed the correct answer to her next question. "Do you still feel the same?" she whispered.

There couldn't have been anything more sincere than the look in Wade's eyes. "Yes."

Only the vague memory of the crowd kept Bronwynn from launching herself into his arms. "I love you too," she murmured around the knot in her throat.

She wished now she hadn't called the reporters in. Bringing them along had seemed like a good idea at the time, but when awareness of the man seated next to her uncurled deep inside her, she wished they would go sensationalize someone else's life. She had a congressman to seduce. Already her imagination was conjuring up images of her loosening the knot in his proper paisley tie.

"What was that, Ms. Pierson?" a reporter asked from the back of the room. "We can't hear you back here."

"I said, I have just one more question for Congressman Grayson." Bronwynn swallowed hard and turned to Wade once again. For a fleeting second, she almost chickened out and asked for directions to Kokomo instead. But from somewhere deep down she drew the strength she needed. He was the man she loved, the man she had waited all her life to love. She wanted him in her life, and all she had to do was ask. "Wade, will you marry me?"

While cameras went off in a frenzy, Wade stared at her, his mind utterly blank for all of five seconds. Bronwynn wanted to marry him? "What about Foxfire? We couldn't live there, you know."

"I know. But it'll make a nice place to go on vacation, won't it?"

"Yeah." He smiled, rising from his chair. The sooner they got away from their audience the better. Taking Bronwynn's hands in his, he pulled her to her feet, his gaze never letting go of hers. "Do you think it can work? We're very different."

"Like night and day," she said with a gentle smile.

"We don't agree on anything."

"Yes, we do," she said, inching closer to him.

Wade shook his head. "No, we don't."

"We agree on this." Without any thought to who was watching, Bronwynn pulled her glasses off and wrapped her arms around Wade's neck. She lifted her mouth to his and kissed him slowly, thoroughly, letting the heat build between them until she knew she'd lose control if she didn't step back.

Wade let her lips part from his reluctantly. Breathlessly he murmured, "You've got a point there."

"So," she said, trying to sound matter-of-fact when her heart was racing and her respiration was faulty at best, "will you marry me?"

He didn't realize how long his answer was in coming. He was too caught up in looking at Bronwynn. He remembered well enough how she had looked in a wedding gown. Possessiveness surged through him as he thought that next time she would be wearing it for him. And when he took it off her, she wasn't going to swear off *all* men; he would be the exception. She would be his to fight with and play with and love. She would see to it he had a balance in his life, and he would see to it she stayed away from power tools.

"Gee, Wade," Bronwynn said dryly, her brows drawing together in annoyance, "just take your time answering. There are only about a million people watching on their TV sets at home. Read my lips this time—will you marry me?"

Wade grinned and pulled her into his embrace. "As long as you don't insist on taking that sheep along on the honeymoon."

Safe and warm in his arms, Bronwynn smiled impishly against his chest. "We'll talk about it."

THE EDITOR'S CORNER

This coming month brings to mind lions and lambs—not only in terms of the weather, but also in terms of our six delightful LOVESWEPTs. You'll find fierce and feisty, tame and gentle characters in our books next month who add up to a rich and exciting array of folks whose stories of falling in love are enthralling.

First, hold on to your hat as a really hot wind blows through chilly London town in Fayrene Preston's marvelous *The Pearls of Sharah II: RAINE'S STORY*, LOVESWEPT #318. When Raine Bennett realized someone was following her through foggy Hyde Park one night, she ran . . . straight into the arms of Michael Carr. He was a stranger who radiated danger and mystery—yet he was a man Raine instinctively knew she could trust. Michael was utterly captivated by her, but the magnificent strand of perfect pearls draped across her exquisite body complicated things. What was she doing with the legendary Pearls of Sharah, which had just been reported stolen to his branch of Interpol? What were her secrets and would she threaten his integrity . . . as well as his heart? This is a dazzling love story you just can't let yourself miss! (Do remember that the Doubleday hardcover edition is available at the same time the paperback is in the stores. Don't miss this chance to collect all three Pearls of Sharah romances in these beautifully bound editions at only $12.95.)

Jan Hudson's **THE RIGHT MOVES**, LOVESWEPT #319, will set your senses ablaze. Jan created two unique characters in her heroine and hero; they were yin and yang, fire and ice, and they could not stay away from each other no matter how hard they tried. Chris Ponder was a spitfire, a dynamo with a temper . . . and with a tow truck. When she took one look at Nick Russo's bedroom eyes, her insides turned to tapioca, and she suddenly wanted to flirt with the danger he represented. But good sense started to prevail. After all, she hardly needed to fall for a handsome charmer who might be all flash and no substance. Still Nick teased, and she felt she might go up in flames . . . especially on one moonlit night that filled her with wonder. This is a breathlessly exciting romance!

In LOVESWEPT #320, **THE SILVER BULLET AFFAIR**, Sandra Chastain shows us once again that love sure can conquer all. When John Garmon learned that his brother Jeffrey's will instructed him to "Take care of Caitlan and the

(continued)

baby—it's mine," he immediately sought out the quicksilver lady who had charmed him at every former meeting. Caitlan proved to be like a fine perfume—good at disappearing and very elusive. She believed that John was her adversary, a villain, perhaps, who might take her baby away if he learned the truth. So how could she lose herself in the hot shivery sensations of his embrace? Bewitched by this fragile woman who broke all the rules, John grows determined to rescue Caitlan from her free-spirited life and the gang of crazy but caring friends who never leave them alone to learn to love each other. A shimmering, vivid love story that we think you'll find a real delight.

The brilliant . . . fun . . . thrilling . . . surprising conclusion to the "Hagen Strikes Again" series, by Kay Hooper, **ACES HIGH,** LOVESWEPT #321, comes your way next month. Skye Prescott was tall, dark, and dangerous, a man who'd never forgotten how Katrina Keller had betrayed him years before. In a world where survival depended on suspicion, he'd fallen in love—and it had broken him as violence never had. When the beautiful redheaded ghost from his past reappeared in his life, Skye was filled with fury, hurt, a desire for revenge—and an aching hunger to make Katrina burn for him again. Katrina had fought her memories, but once she was in his arms, she couldn't fight him or her own primal passion. She was his match, his mate—but belonging to him body and spirit gave him the power to destroy her. When Skye faced his most violent enemy, Trina knew she faced the most desperate gamble of her life. Now, friends, need I tease you with the fact that Hagen also gets his in this fabulous book? I know you've been wondering (as all of us here have) what Kay was going to do for that paunchy devil in terms of a love story. Well, next month you will know. And I can guarantee that Kay has been as delightfully inventive as we had hoped and dreamed she would be.

Please give a great, warm welcome to talented new author Marcia Evanick by getting and enjoying her powerfully emotional romance, **PERFECT MORNING,** LOVESWEPT #322. How this story will touch your heart! When Jason Nesbit entered Riki McCormick's front yard in search of his young daughter, he never expected to find an emerald-eyed vixen as her foster mother. He had just learned that he had a child when his ex-wife died in an accident. Traumatized after her mother's death, the girl had not spoken since. Jason marveled at Riki's houseful of love—and was capti-

(continued)

vated by the sweet, spirited woman who'd made room in her life for so many special children. Under Jason's steamy scrutiny, Riki felt a wave of longing to be kissed breathless and held tight. When his Texas drawl warned her that her waiting days were over, she unpacked her slinkiest lingerie and dreamed of satin sheets and firelight. But courting Riki with seven children around seemed downright impossible. You'll laugh and cry with Jason and Riki as they try to make everyone happy. A keeper!

Halsey Morgan is alive—and Stevie Lee wanted him dead. What a way to open a romance! Glenna McReynolds has created two wonderful, thrilling characters in LOVESWEPT #323, **STEVIE LEE.** Halsey Morgan was Stevie Lee's long-lost neighbor. She had plotted for the last few years to buy his cabin for his back taxes, sell it for a huge profit, and get out of her small town so she could see the world. Handsome Halsey had blazed a trail of adventure from the Himalayas to the Amazon—and was thought to be dead. Now he was back—ruining her plans to escape and melting her with sizzling kisses that almost made her forget why she'd ever wanted to go away. His wildness excited her senses to riot, while his husky voice made her tremble with want. Hal had never stayed anywhere long enough to fall in love, but Stevie was the answer to a loneliness he'd never dared admit. He made her take chances, climb mountains, and taught her how to love him. But could Hal persuade her to risk loving him and follow her dreams while held tight in his arms? Don't miss this great story . . . which, we think you'll agree, knocks your socks off!

Enjoy those blustery days next month curled up with six LOVESWEPTs that are as hot as they are happily-ever-after.

Carolyn Nichols

Carolyn Nichols
Editor
LOVESWEPT
Bantam Books
666 Fifth Avenue
New York, NY 10103